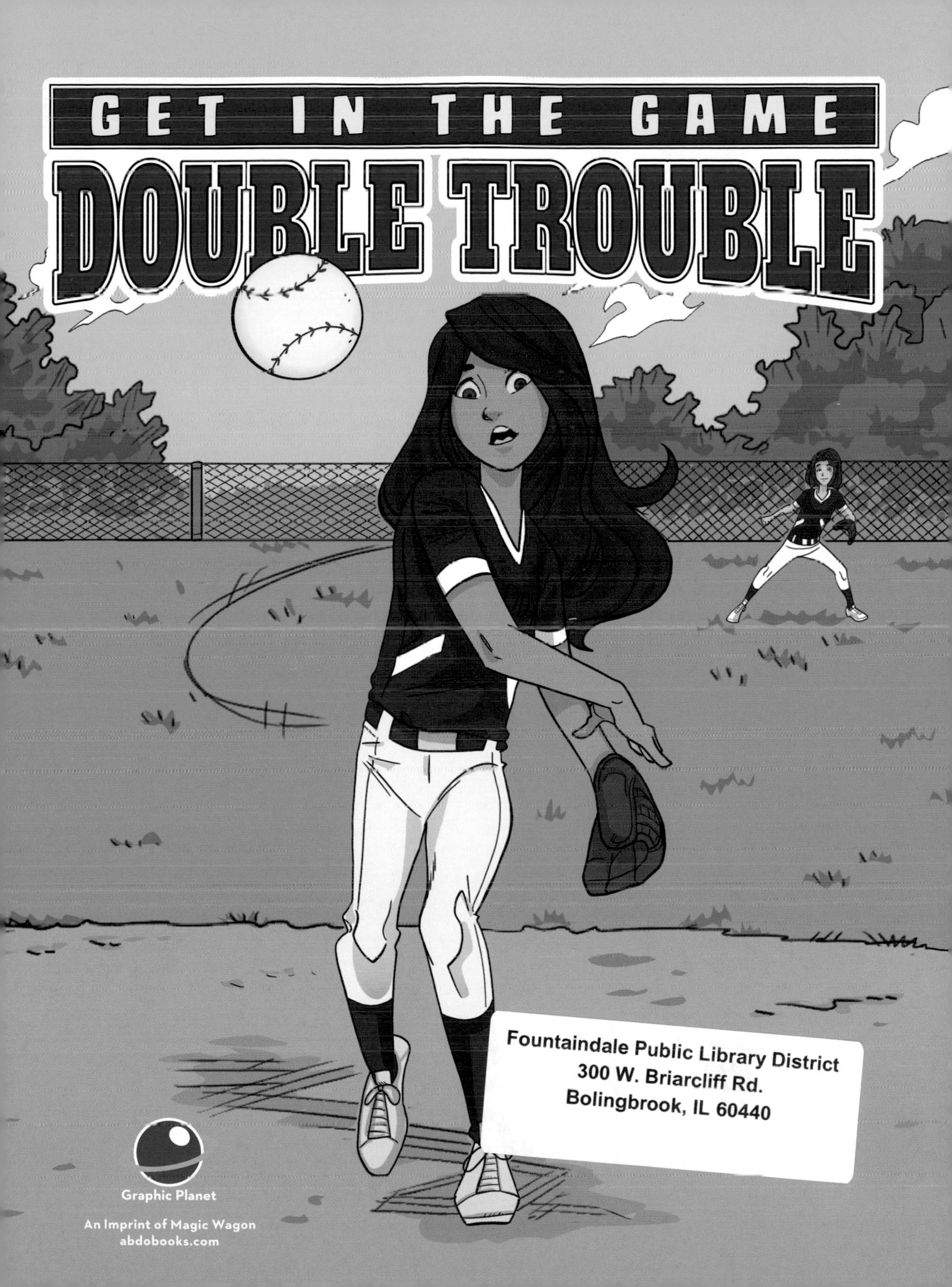
GET IN THE GAME
DOUBLE TROUBLE
Graphic Planet
An Imprint of Magic Wagon
abdobooks.com

abdobooks.com

Published by Magic Wagon, a division of ABDO, PO Box 398166, Minneapolis, Minnesota 55439.
Copyright © 2021 by Abdo Consulting Group, Inc. International copyrights reserved in all countries.
No part of this book may be reproduced in any form without written permission from the publisher.
Graphic Planet™ is a trademark and logo of Magic Wagon.

Printed in the United States of America, North Mankato, Minnesota.
082020
012021

Written by Bill Yu
Illustrated by Eduardo Garcia
Colored by Sebastian Garcia
Lettered by Kathryn S. Renta
Layout and design by Michelle Principe and Pejee Calanog of Glass House Graphics
  and Christina Doffing of ABDO
Editorial supervision by David Campiti
Packaged by Glass House Graphics
Art Directed by Candice Keimig and Laura Graphenteen
Editorial Support by Tamara L. Britton

Library of Congress Control Number: 2020930663

Publisher's Cataloging-in-Publication Data

Names: Yu, Bill, author. | Garcia, Eduardo; Garcia, Sebastian, illustrators.
Title: Double trouble / by Bill Yu ; illustrated by Eduardo Garcia and Sebastian Garcia.
Description: Minneapolis, Minnesota : Magic Wagon, 2021. | Series: Get in the game
Summary: Isabella Clemente plays second base on Peabody's softball team. The team has won two
    championships in a row! But this season the team is faltering. When Isabella lashes out at her
    teammates, Coach Dawson points out that it is easy to be a good sport on a winning team. Can
    Isabella support her team when its season will be a losing one? What does she truly value?
Identifiers: ISBN 9781532138300 (lib. bdg.) | ISBN 9781644944790 (pbk.) | ISBN 9781532139024
    (ebook) | ISBN 9781532139383 (Read-to-Me ebook)
Subjects: LCSH: Softball--Juvenile fiction. | Sports teams--Juvenile fiction. | Winning and losing--
    Juvenile fiction. | Sportsmanship--Juvenile fiction. | Friendship--Juvenile fiction
Classification: DDC [741.5]--dc23

CONTENTS

DOUBLE TROUBLE

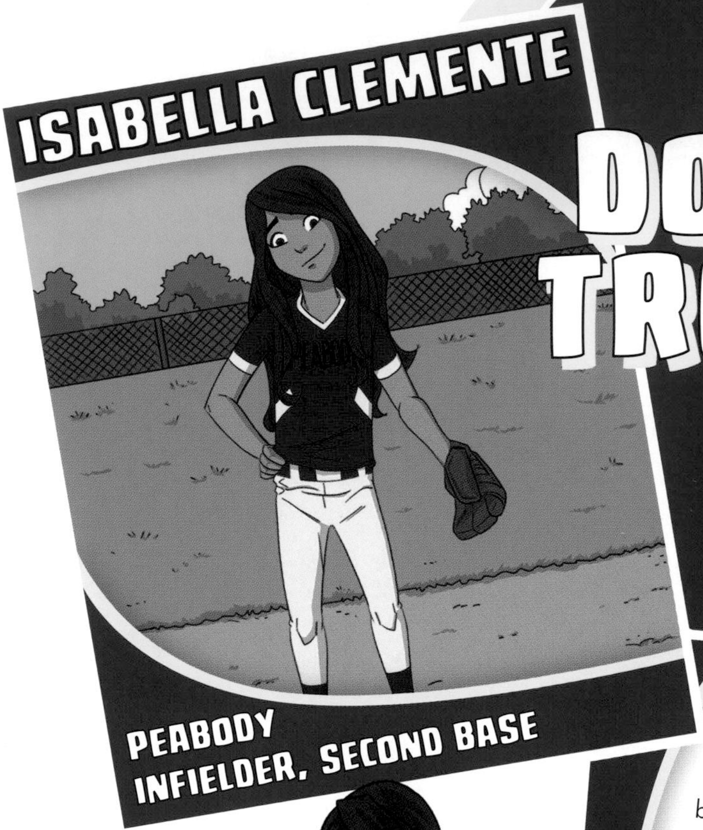
ISABELLA CLEMENTE
PEABODY
INFIELDER, SECOND BASE

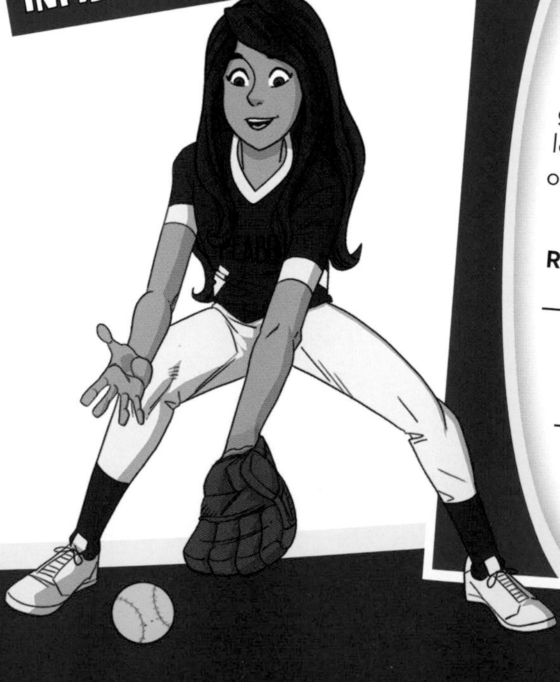

ISABELLA CLEMENTE,
Infielder, Second Base #21

Isabella Clemente plays second base for the Peabody's softball team. She leads the Highlanders with passion, hustle, and love of the game. She wears # 21 in honor of legendary Puerto Rican baseball outfielder, Roberto Clemente.

RECORD

GAMES	AT BATS	HITS
10	32	15

HOME RUNS	BATTING AVG	RBI
7	.469	21

ISABELLA CLEMENTE

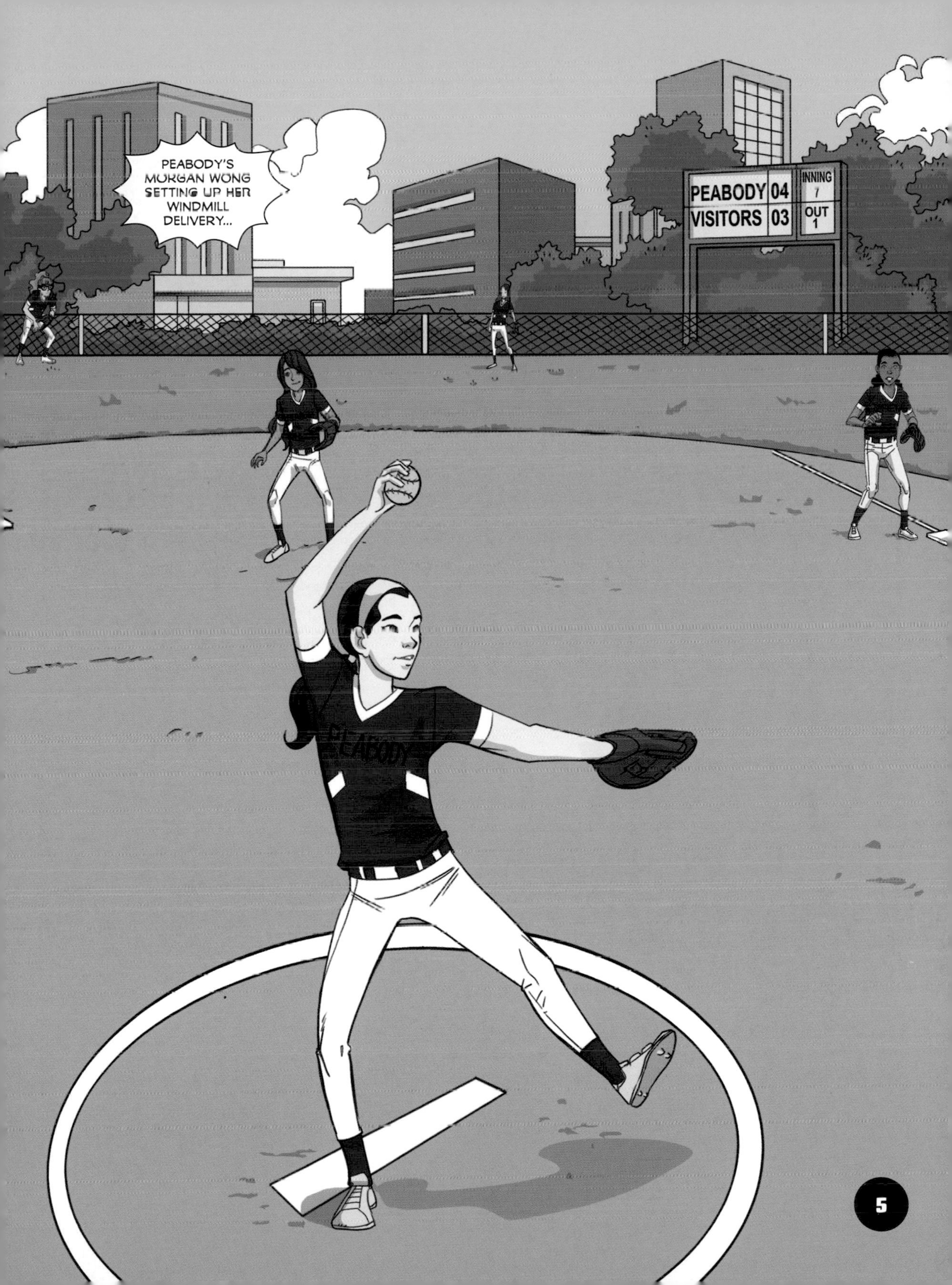
PEABODY'S MORGAN WONG SETTING UP HER WINDMILL DELIVERY...
PEABODY 04
VISITORS 03
INNING 7
OUT 1
PEABODY

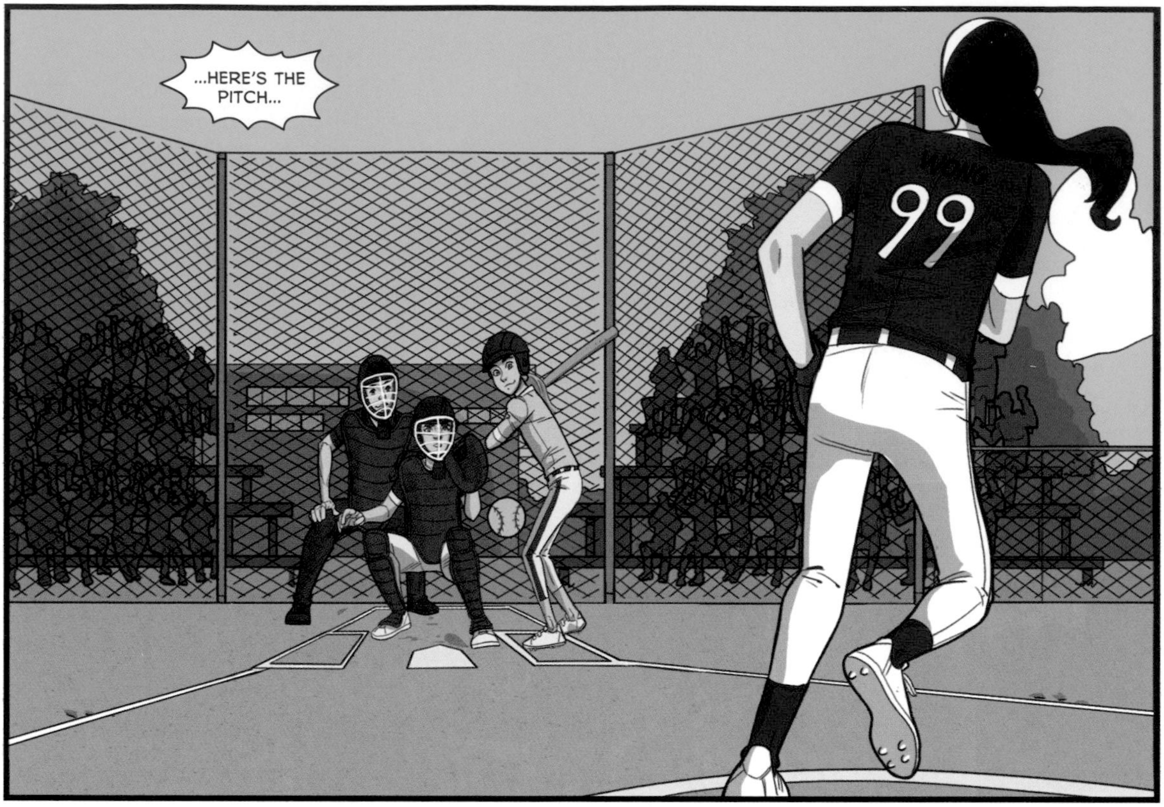
...HERE'S THE PITCH...
WONG
99

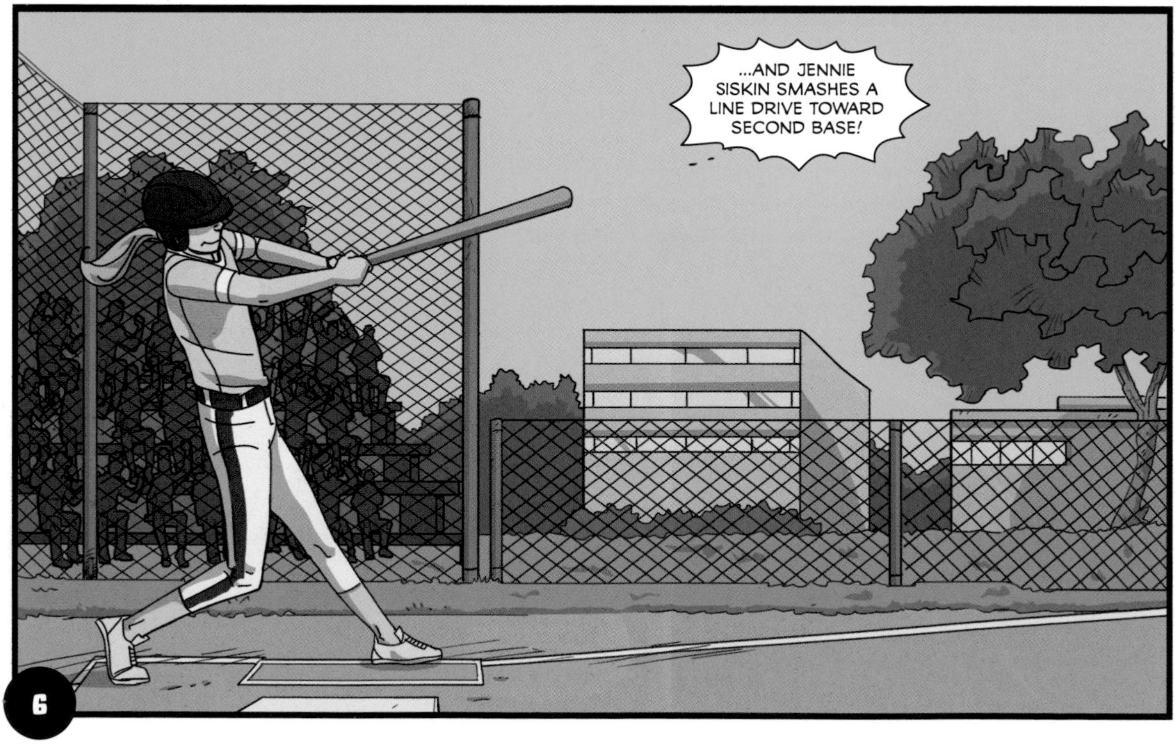
...AND JENNIE SISKIN SMASHES A LINE DRIVE TOWARD SECOND BASE!

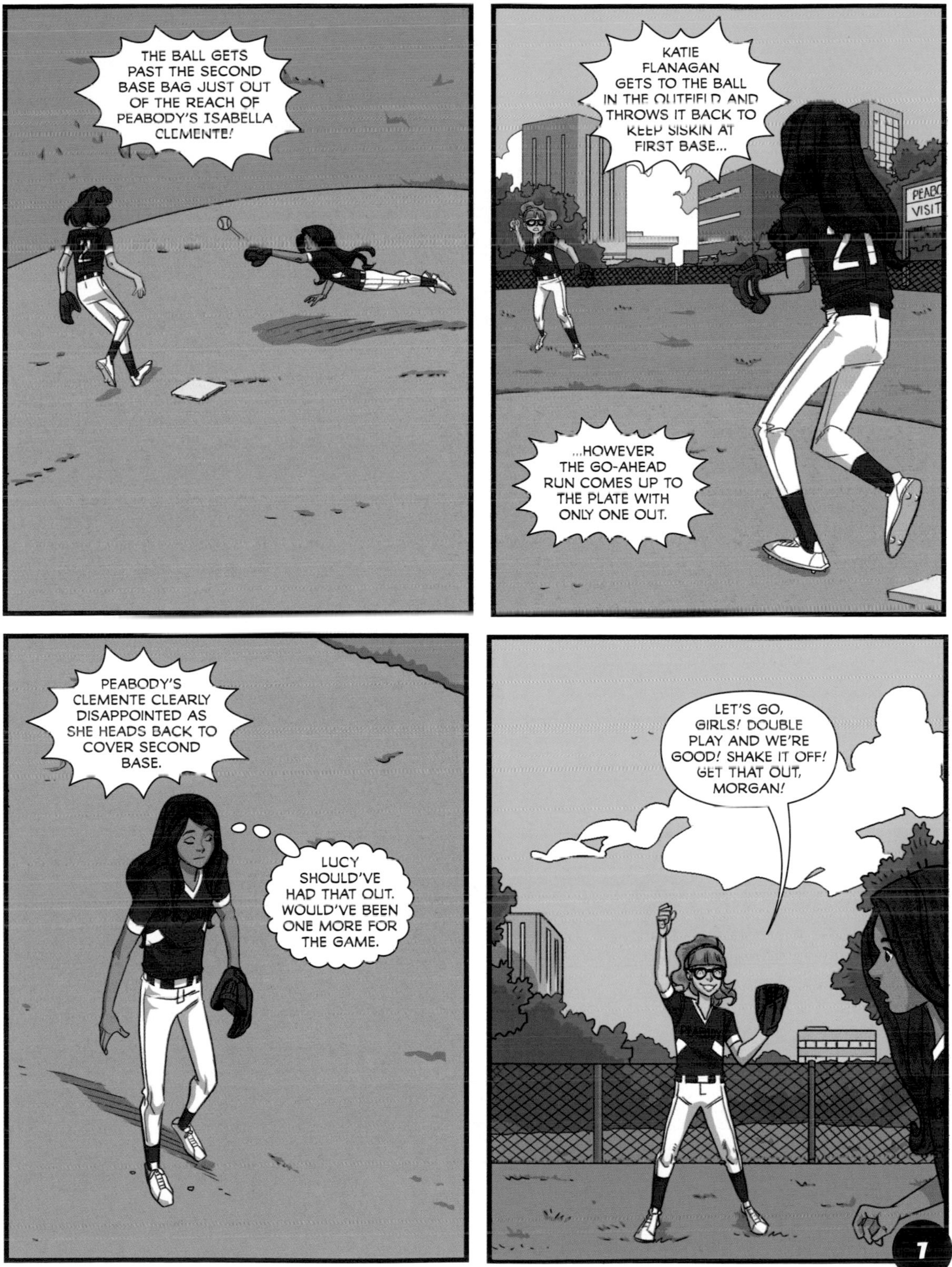
THE BALL GETS PAST THE SECOND BASE BAG JUST OUT OF THE REACH OF PEABODY'S ISABELLA CLEMENTE!
KATIE FLANAGAN GETS TO THE BALL IN THE OUTFIELD AND THROWS IT BACK TO KEEP SISKIN AT FIRST BASE...
PEABO
VISIT
...HOWEVER THE GO-AHEAD RUN COMES UP TO THE PLATE WITH ONLY ONE OUT.
PEABODY'S CLEMENTE CLEARLY DISAPPOINTED AS SHE HEADS BACK TO COVER SECOND BASE.
LUCY SHOULD'VE HAD THAT OUT. WOULD'VE BEEN ONE MORE FOR THE GAME.
LET'S GO, GIRLS! DOUBLE PLAY AND WE'RE GOOD! SHAKE IT OFF! GET THAT OUT, MORGAN!

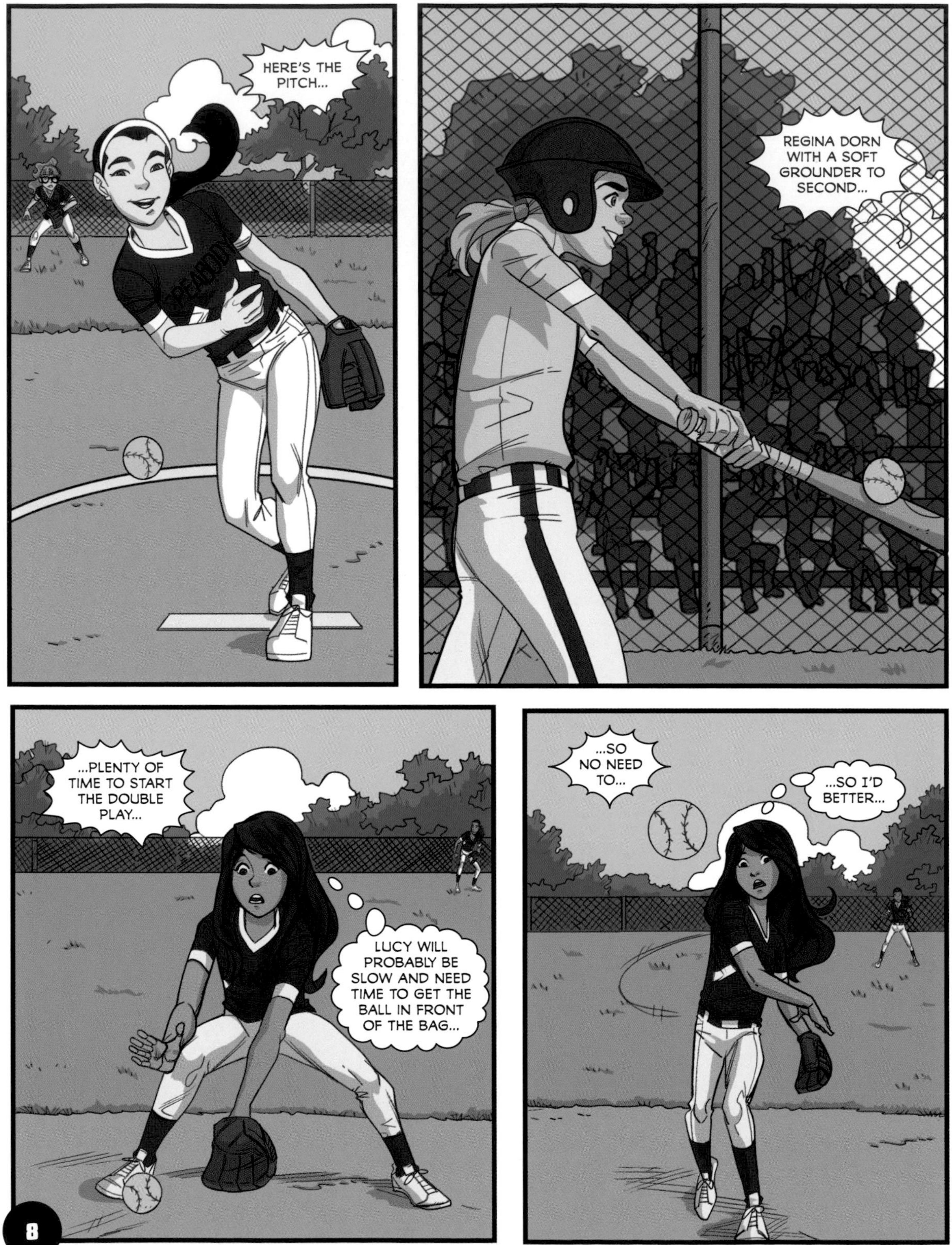
HERE'S THE PITCH...
REGINA DORN WITH A SOFT GROUNDER TO SECOND...
...PLENTY OF TIME TO START THE DOUBLE PLAY...
LUCY WILL PROBABLY BE SLOW AND NEED TIME TO GET THE BALL IN FRONT OF THE BAG...
...SO NO NEED TO...
...SO I'D BETTER...

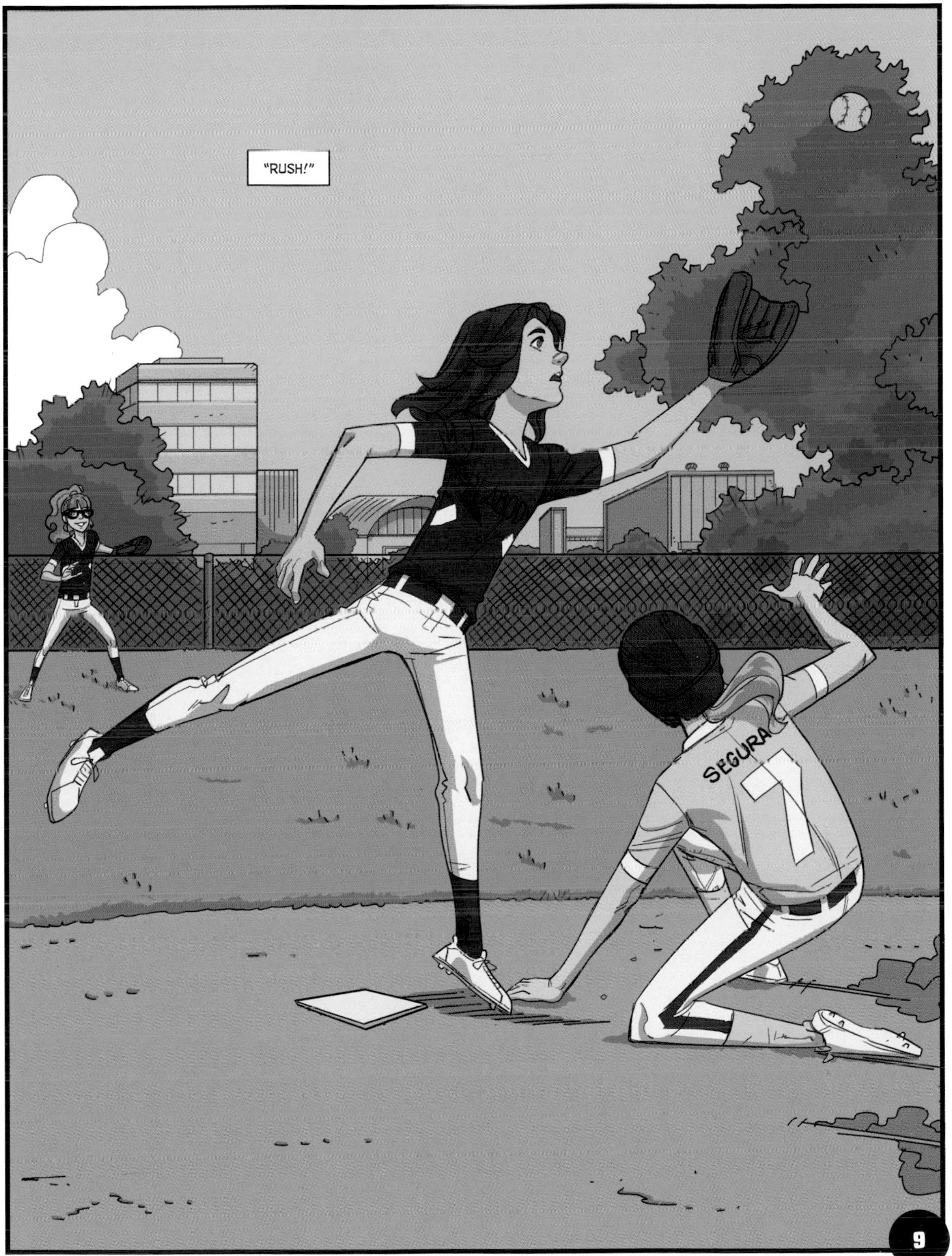
"RUSH!"
SEGURA
7

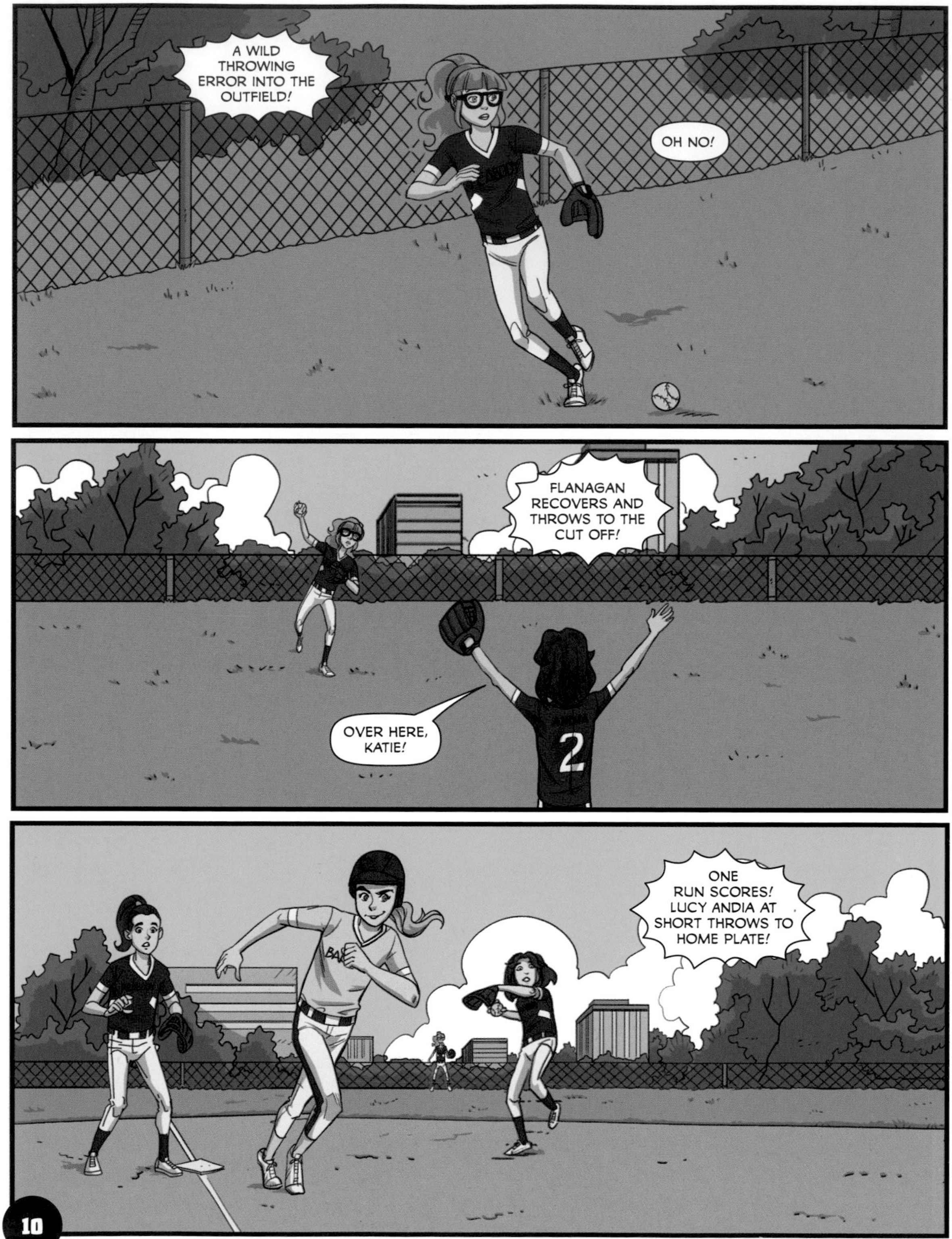
A WILD THROWING ERROR INTO THE OUTFIELD!
OH NO!
FLANAGAN RECOVERS AND THROWS TO THE CUT OFF!
OVER HERE, KATIE!
2
ONE RUN SCORES! LUCY ANDIA AT SHORT THROWS TO HOME PLATE!

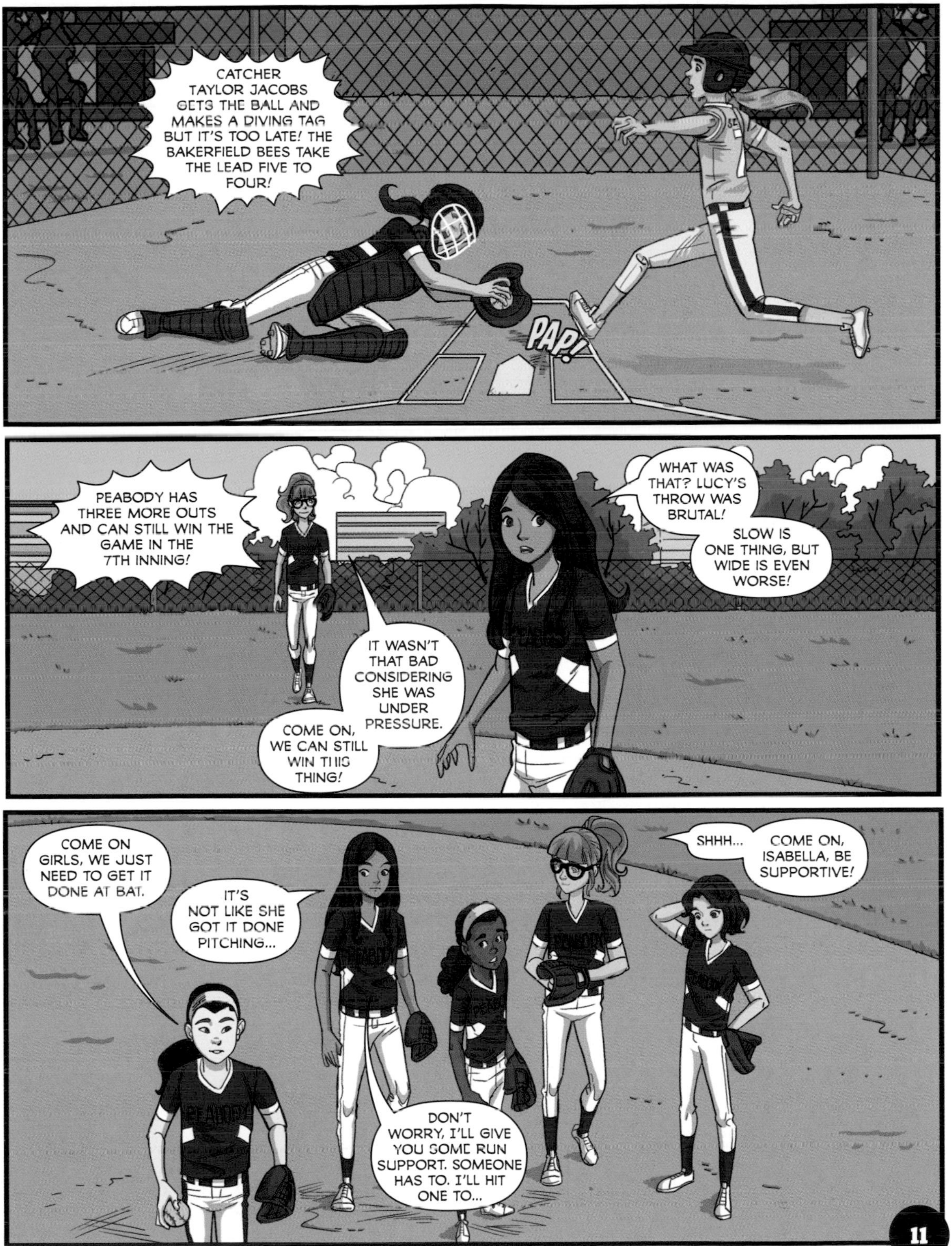
CATCHER TAYLOR JACOBS GETS THE BALL AND MAKES A DIVING TAG BUT IT'S TOO LATE! THE BAKERFIELD BEES TAKE THE LEAD FIVE TO FOUR!
PAP!
PEABODY HAS THREE MORE OUTS AND CAN STILL WIN THE GAME IN THE 7TH INNING!
WHAT WAS THAT? LUCY'S THROW WAS BRUTAL!
SLOW IS ONE THING, BUT WIDE IS EVEN WORSE!
IT WASN'T THAT BAD CONSIDERING SHE WAS UNDER PRESSURE.
COME ON, WE CAN STILL WIN THIS THING!
COME ON GIRLS, WE JUST NEED TO GET IT DONE AT BAT.
IT'S NOT LIKE SHE GOT IT DONE PITCHING...
SHHH...
COME ON, ISABELLA, BE SUPPORTIVE!
DON'T WORRY, I'LL GIVE YOU SOME RUN SUPPORT. SOMEONE HAS TO. I'LL HIT ONE TO...

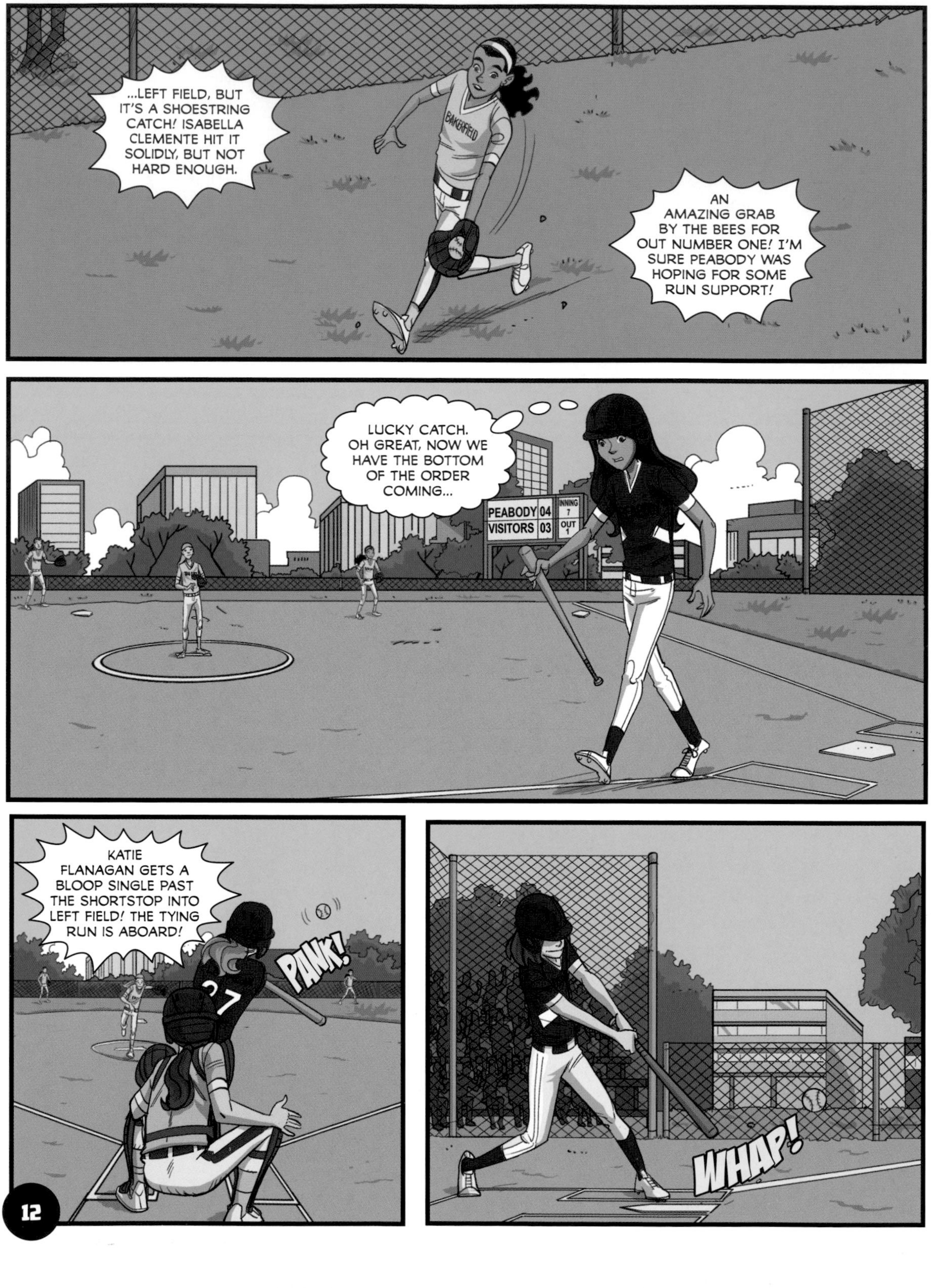
...LEFT FIELD, BUT IT'S A SHOESTRING CATCH! ISABELLA CLEMENTE HIT IT SOLIDLY, BUT NOT HARD ENOUGH.
BAKERFIELD
AN AMAZING GRAB BY THE BEES FOR OUT NUMBER ONE! I'M SURE PEABODY WAS HOPING FOR SOME RUN SUPPORT!
LUCKY CATCH. OH GREAT, NOW WE HAVE THE BOTTOM OF THE ORDER COMING...
PEABODY 04 INNING 7
VISITORS 03 OUT 1
KATIE FLANAGAN GETS A BLOOP SINGLE PAST THE SHORTSTOP INTO LEFT FIELD! THE TYING RUN IS ABOARD!
27
PANK!
WHAP!

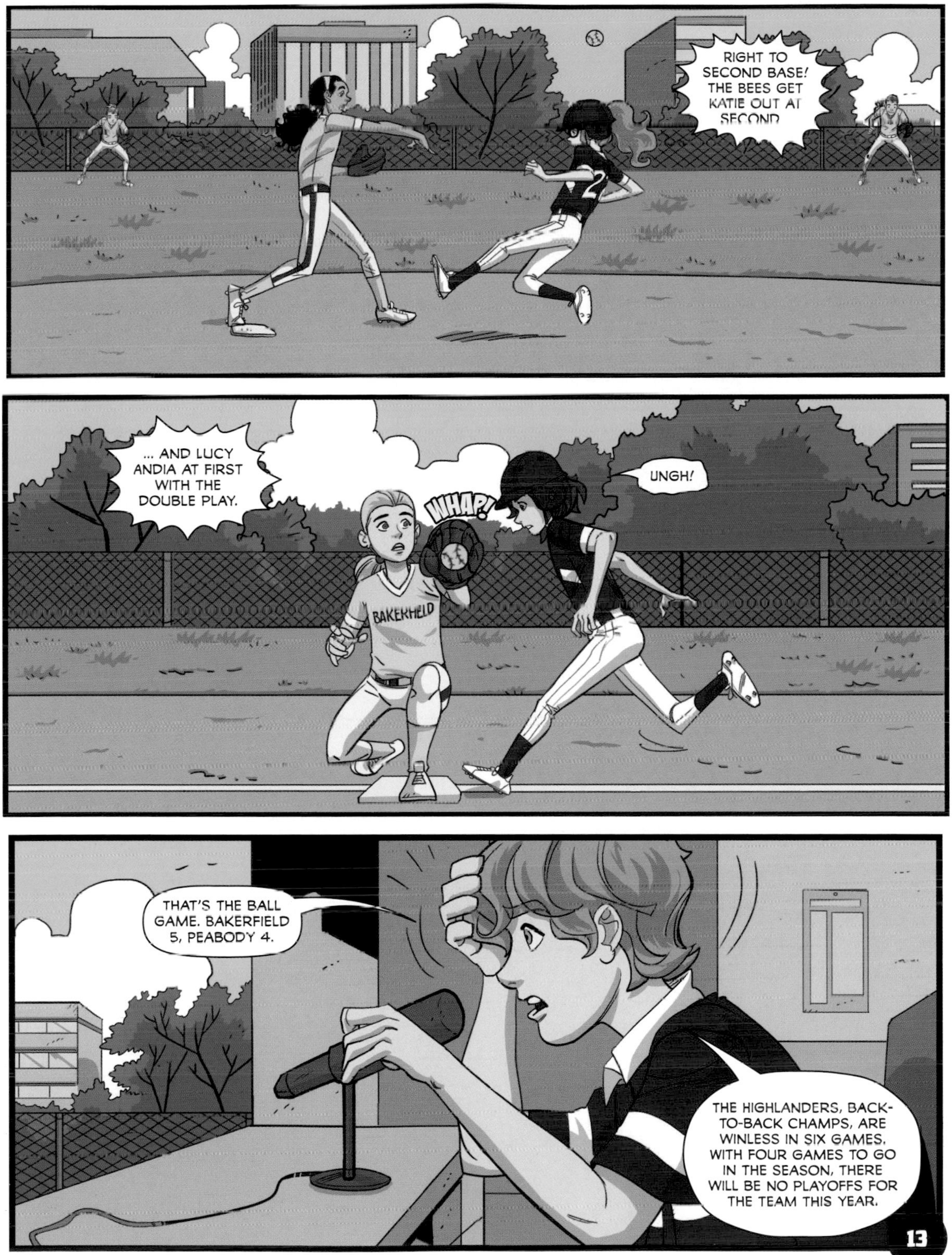
RIGHT TO SECOND BASE! THE BEES GET KATIE OUT AT SECOND
... AND LUCY ANDIA AT FIRST WITH THE DOUBLE PLAY.
WHAP!
UNGH!
BAKERFIELD
THAT'S THE BALL GAME. BAKERFIELD 5, PEABODY 4.
THE HIGHLANDERS, BACK-TO-BACK CHAMPS, ARE WINLESS IN SIX GAMES. WITH FOUR GAMES TO GO IN THE SEASON, THERE WILL BE NO PLAYOFFS FOR THE TEAM THIS YEAR.

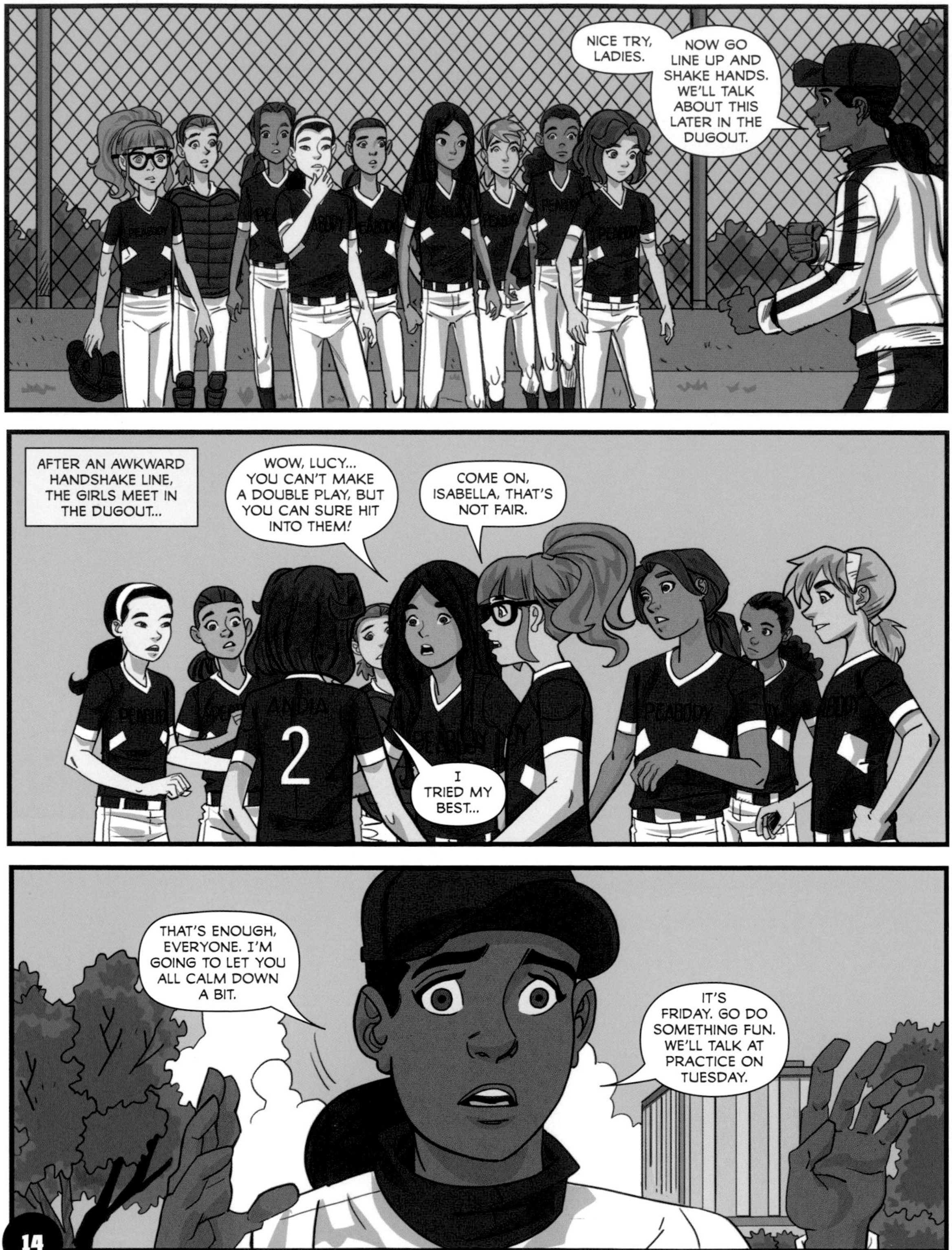
NICE TRY, LADIES.
NOW GO LINE UP AND SHAKE HANDS. WE'LL TALK ABOUT THIS LATER IN THE DUGOUT.
AFTER AN AWKWARD HANDSHAKE LINE, THE GIRLS MEET IN THE DUGOUT...
WOW, LUCY... YOU CAN'T MAKE A DOUBLE PLAY, BUT YOU CAN SURE HIT INTO THEM!
COME ON, ISABELLA, THAT'S NOT FAIR.
I TRIED MY BEST...
THAT'S ENOUGH, EVERYONE. I'M GOING TO LET YOU ALL CALM DOWN A BIT.
IT'S FRIDAY. GO DO SOMETHING FUN. WE'LL TALK AT PRACTICE ON TUESDAY.

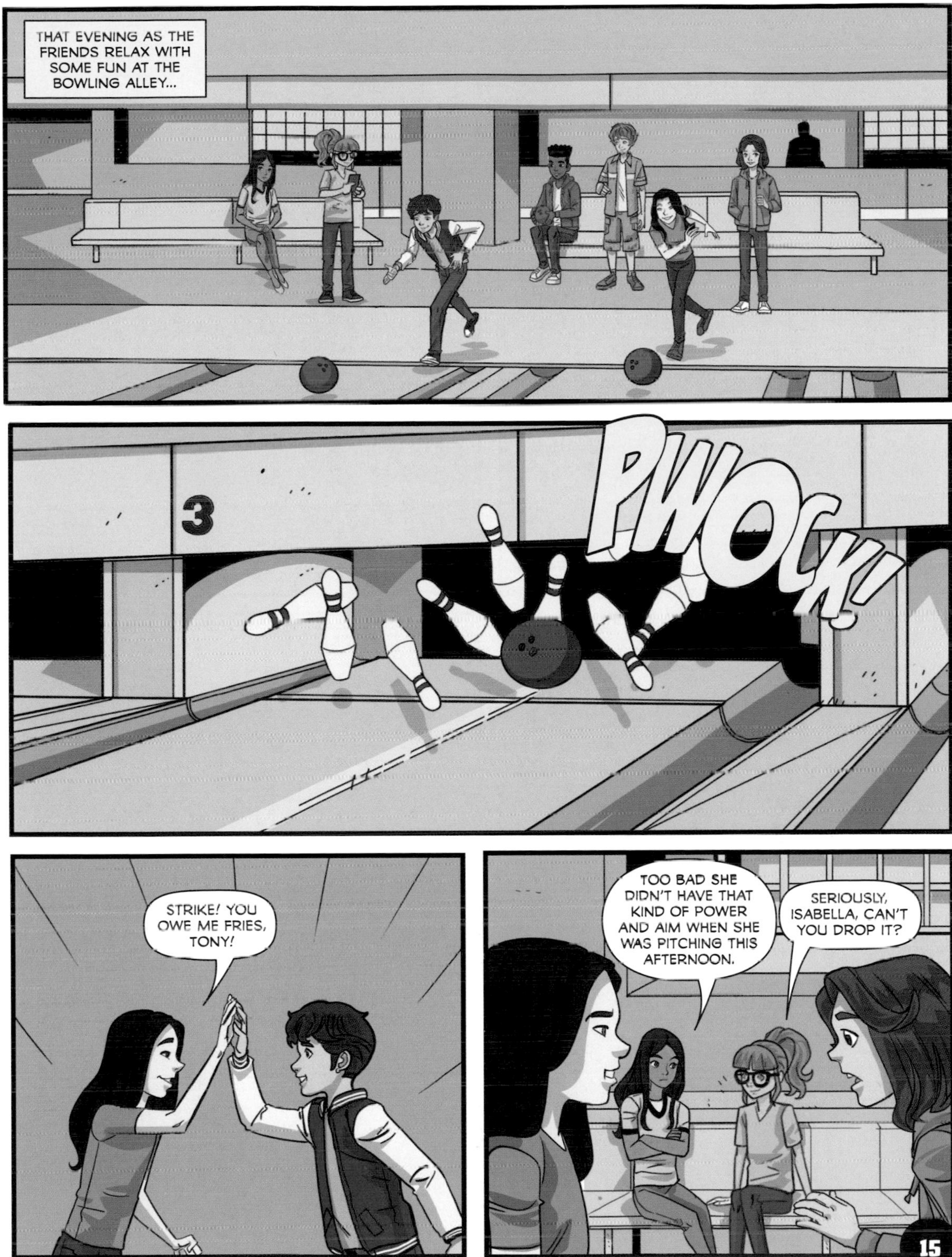
THAT EVENING AS THE FRIENDS RELAX WITH SOME FUN AT THE BOWLING ALLEY...
3
PWOCK!
STRIKE! YOU OWE ME FRIES, TONY!
TOO BAD SHE DIDN'T HAVE THAT KIND OF POWER AND AIM WHEN SHE WAS PITCHING THIS AFTERNOON.
SERIOUSLY, ISABELLA, CAN'T YOU DROP IT?

HEY IS, WHAT'S YOUR DEAL?

COME ON, ISABELLA, CAN'T YOU JUST FORGET ABOUT THE GAME AND HAVE SOME FUN?

YOU WEREN'T ANY BETTER, LUCY!

IF YOU'D MADE SOME PLAYS IN THE INFIELD WE'D HAVE WON!

I GAVE YOU A PERFECT THROW TO TURN THE DOUBLE PLAY AND YOU LET IT GO INTO CENTER FIELD!

IT WAS ACTUALLY HIGH, ISABELLA...

I DON'T NEED THIS. I'M OUT OF HERE. TONY, YOU CAN GET ME THOSE FRIES NEXT TIME.

TONY, I WANT TO GO HOME.

HEY KEITH, CAN YOU GO CHECK ON MY SISTER AND TEXT MY MOM TO PICK US UP? I'LL MEET YOU UPSTAIRS.

UH, YEAH SURE THING, TONY.

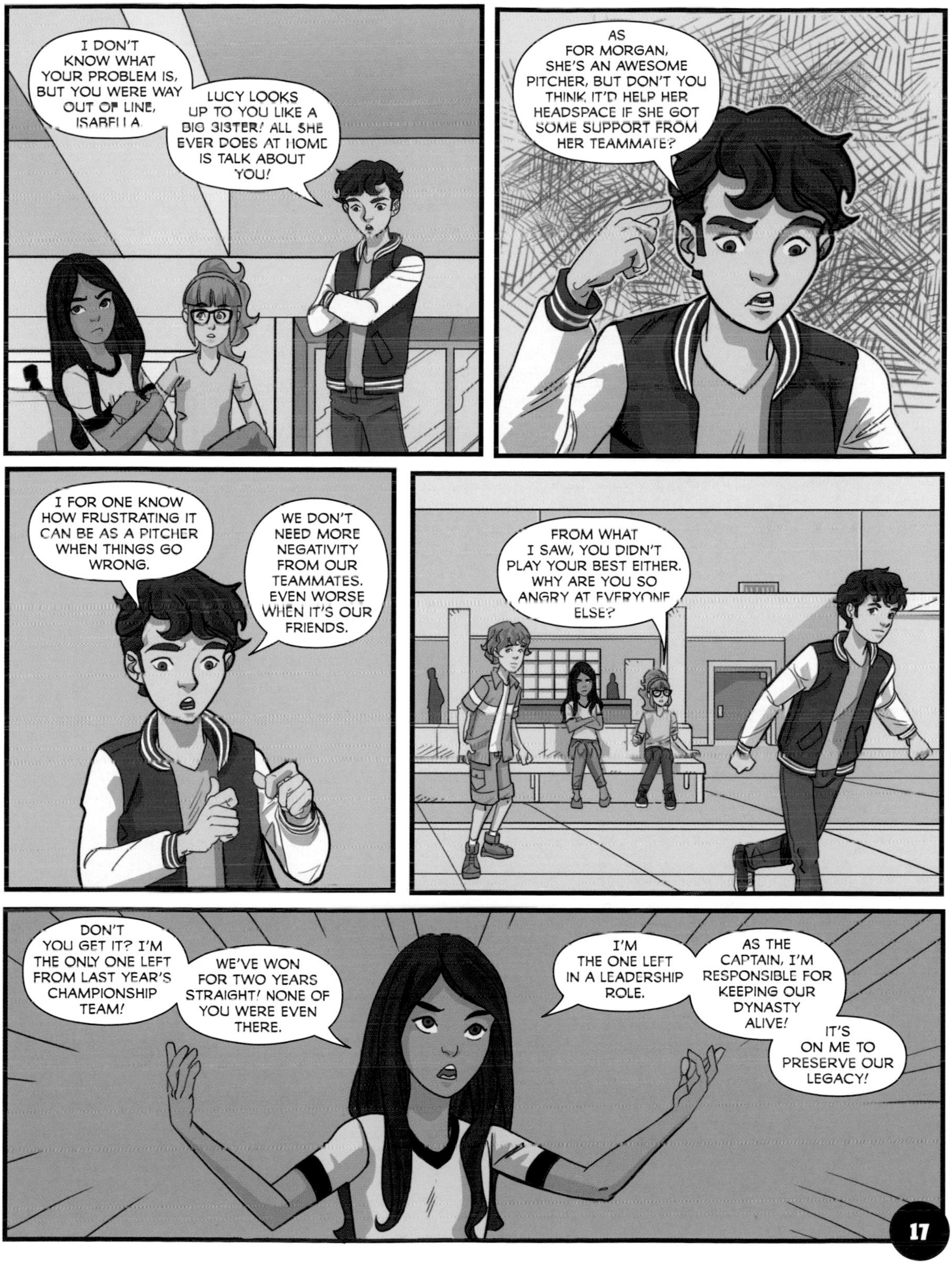
I DON'T KNOW WHAT YOUR PROBLEM IS, BUT YOU WERE WAY OUT OF LINE, ISABELLA.
LUCY LOOKS UP TO YOU LIKE A BIG SISTER! ALL SHE EVER DOES AT HOME IS TALK ABOUT YOU!
AS FOR MORGAN, SHE'S AN AWESOME PITCHER, BUT DON'T YOU THINK IT'D HELP HER HEADSPACE IF SHE GOT SOME SUPPORT FROM HER TEAMMATE?
I FOR ONE KNOW HOW FRUSTRATING IT CAN BE AS A PITCHER WHEN THINGS GO WRONG.
WE DON'T NEED MORE NEGATIVITY FROM OUR TEAMMATES. EVEN WORSE WHEN IT'S OUR FRIENDS.
FROM WHAT I SAW, YOU DIDN'T PLAY YOUR BEST EITHER. WHY ARE YOU SO ANGRY AT EVERYONE ELSE?
DON'T YOU GET IT? I'M THE ONLY ONE LEFT FROM LAST YEAR'S CHAMPIONSHIP TEAM!
WE'VE WON FOR TWO YEARS STRAIGHT! NONE OF YOU WERE EVEN THERE.
I'M THE ONE LEFT IN A LEADERSHIP ROLE.
AS THE CAPTAIN, I'M RESPONSIBLE FOR KEEPING OUR DYNASTY ALIVE!
IT'S ON ME TO PRESERVE OUR LEGACY!

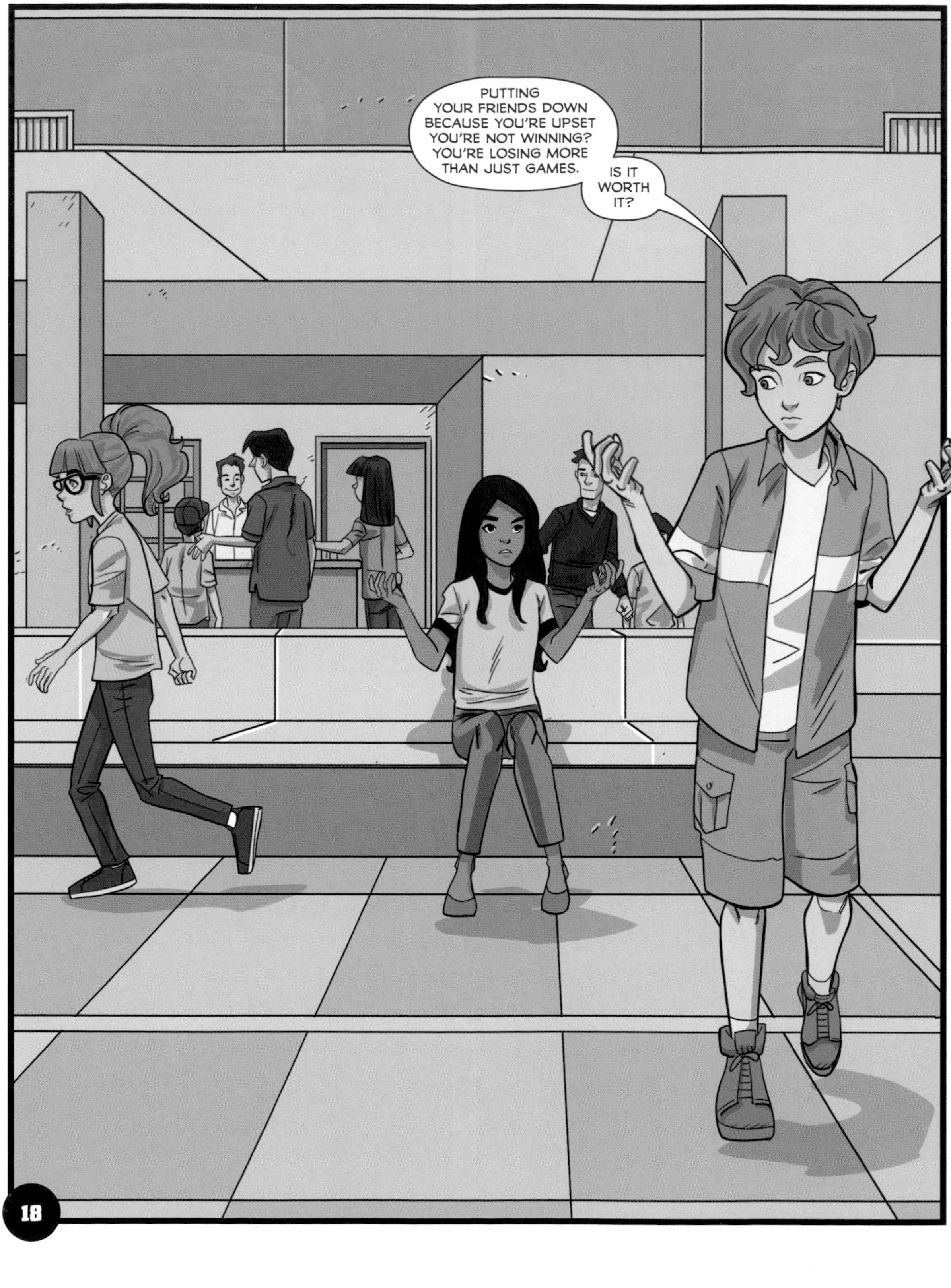
PUTTING YOUR FRIENDS DOWN BECAUSE YOU'RE UPSET YOU'RE NOT WINNING? YOU'RE LOSING MORE THAN JUST GAMES.
IS IT WORTH IT?

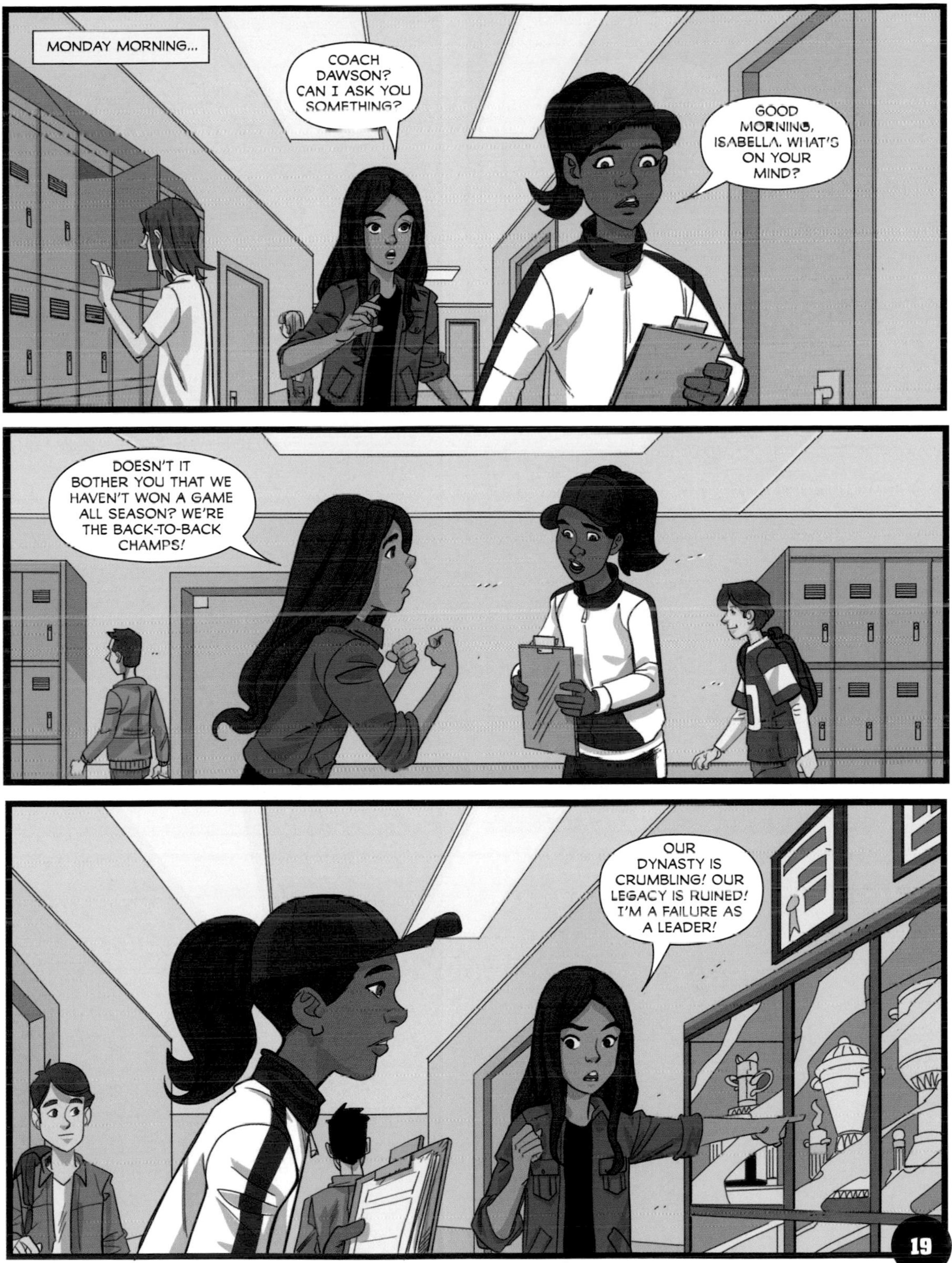
MONDAY MORNING...
COACH DAWSON? CAN I ASK YOU SOMETHING?
GOOD MORNING, ISABELLA. WHAT'S ON YOUR MIND?
DOESN'T IT BOTHER YOU THAT WE HAVEN'T WON A GAME ALL SEASON? WE'RE THE BACK-TO-BACK CHAMPS!
OUR DYNASTY IS CRUMBLING! OUR LEGACY IS RUINED! I'M A FAILURE AS A LEADER!

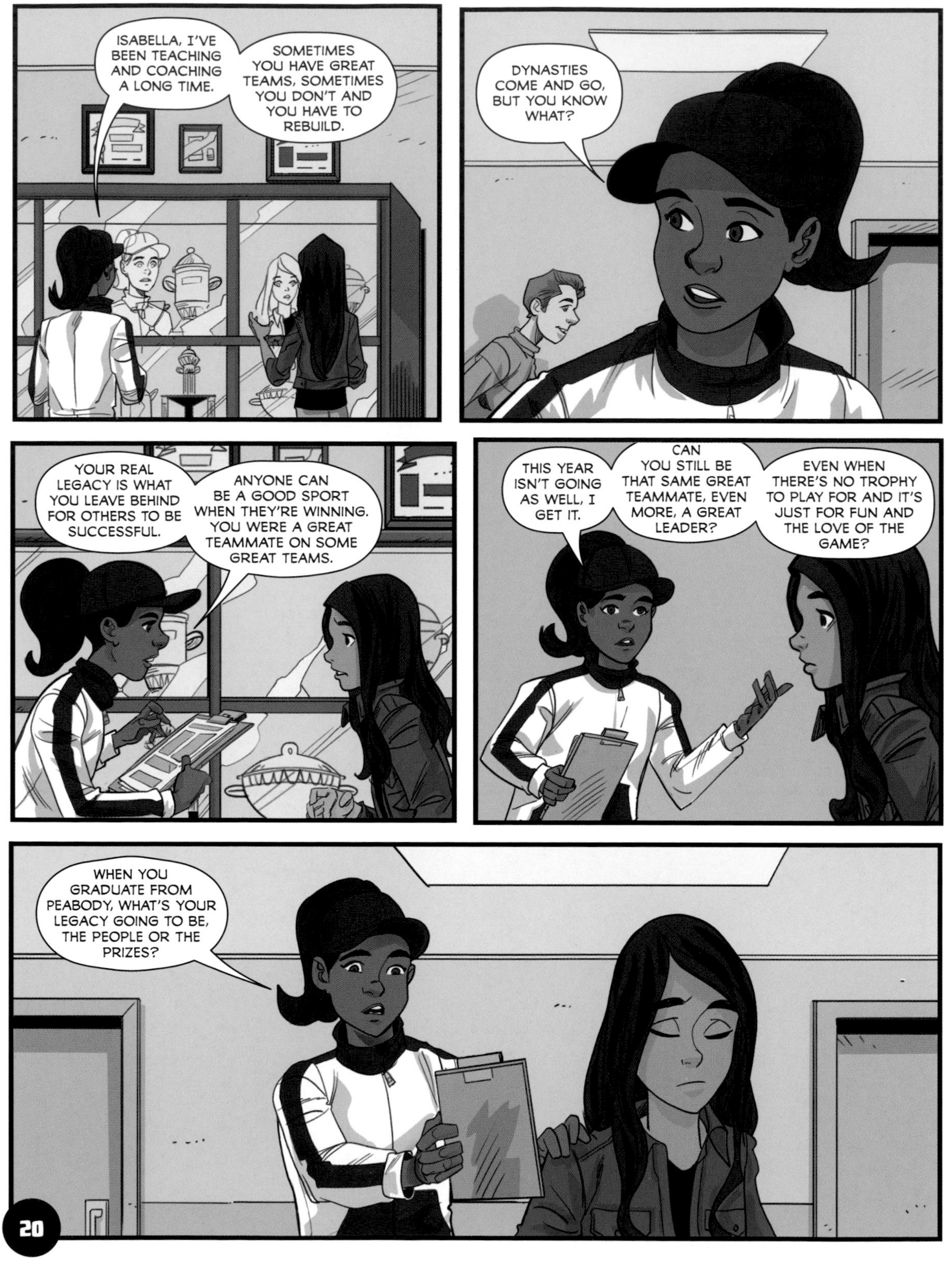
ISABELLA, I'VE BEEN TEACHING AND COACHING A LONG TIME.
SOMETIMES YOU HAVE GREAT TEAMS, SOMETIMES YOU DON'T AND YOU HAVE TO REBUILD.
DYNASTIES COME AND GO, BUT YOU KNOW WHAT?
YOUR REAL LEGACY IS WHAT YOU LEAVE BEHIND FOR OTHERS TO BE SUCCESSFUL.
ANYONE CAN BE A GOOD SPORT WHEN THEY'RE WINNING. YOU WERE A GREAT TEAMMATE ON SOME GREAT TEAMS.
THIS YEAR ISN'T GOING AS WELL, I GET IT.
CAN YOU STILL BE THAT SAME GREAT TEAMMATE, EVEN MORE, A GREAT LEADER?
EVEN WHEN THERE'S NO TROPHY TO PLAY FOR AND IT'S JUST FOR FUN AND THE LOVE OF THE GAME?
WHEN YOU GRADUATE FROM PEABODY, WHAT'S YOUR LEGACY GOING TO BE, THE PEOPLE OR THE PRIZES?

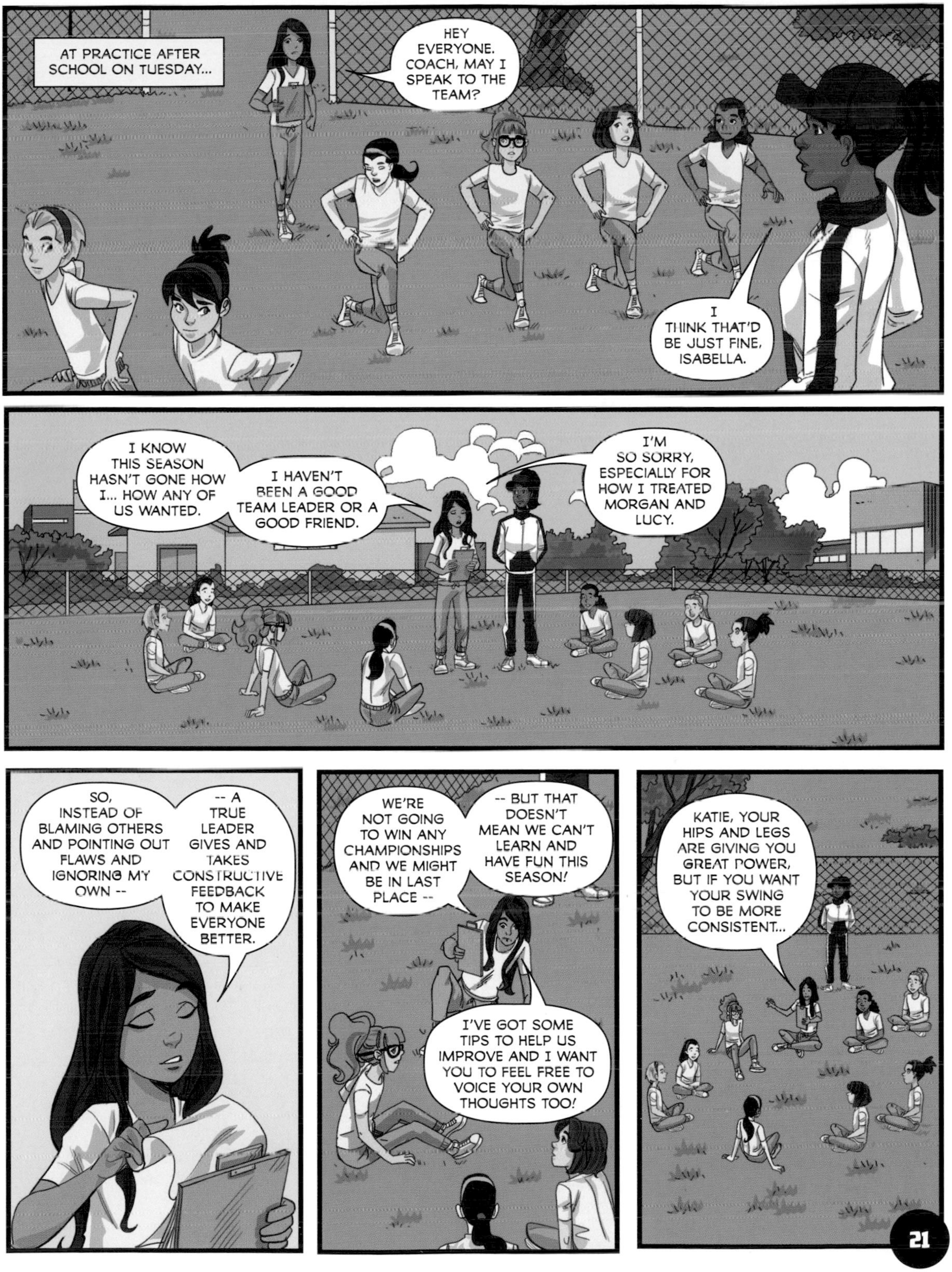
AT PRACTICE AFTER SCHOOL ON TUESDAY...
HEY EVERYONE. COACH, MAY I SPEAK TO THE TEAM?
I THINK THAT'D BE JUST FINE, ISABELLA.
I KNOW THIS SEASON HASN'T GONE HOW I... HOW ANY OF US WANTED.
I HAVEN'T BEEN A GOOD TEAM LEADER OR A GOOD FRIEND.
I'M SO SORRY, ESPECIALLY FOR HOW I TREATED MORGAN AND LUCY.
SO, INSTEAD OF BLAMING OTHERS AND POINTING OUT FLAWS AND IGNORING MY OWN --
-- A TRUE LEADER GIVES AND TAKES CONSTRUCTIVE FEEDBACK TO MAKE EVERYONE BETTER.
WE'RE NOT GOING TO WIN ANY CHAMPIONSHIPS AND WE MIGHT BE IN LAST PLACE --
-- BUT THAT DOESN'T MEAN WE CAN'T LEARN AND HAVE FUN THIS SEASON!
I'VE GOT SOME TIPS TO HELP US IMPROVE AND I WANT YOU TO FEEL FREE TO VOICE YOUR OWN THOUGHTS TOO!
KATIE, YOUR HIPS AND LEGS ARE GIVING YOU GREAT POWER, BUT IF YOU WANT YOUR SWING TO BE MORE CONSISTENT...

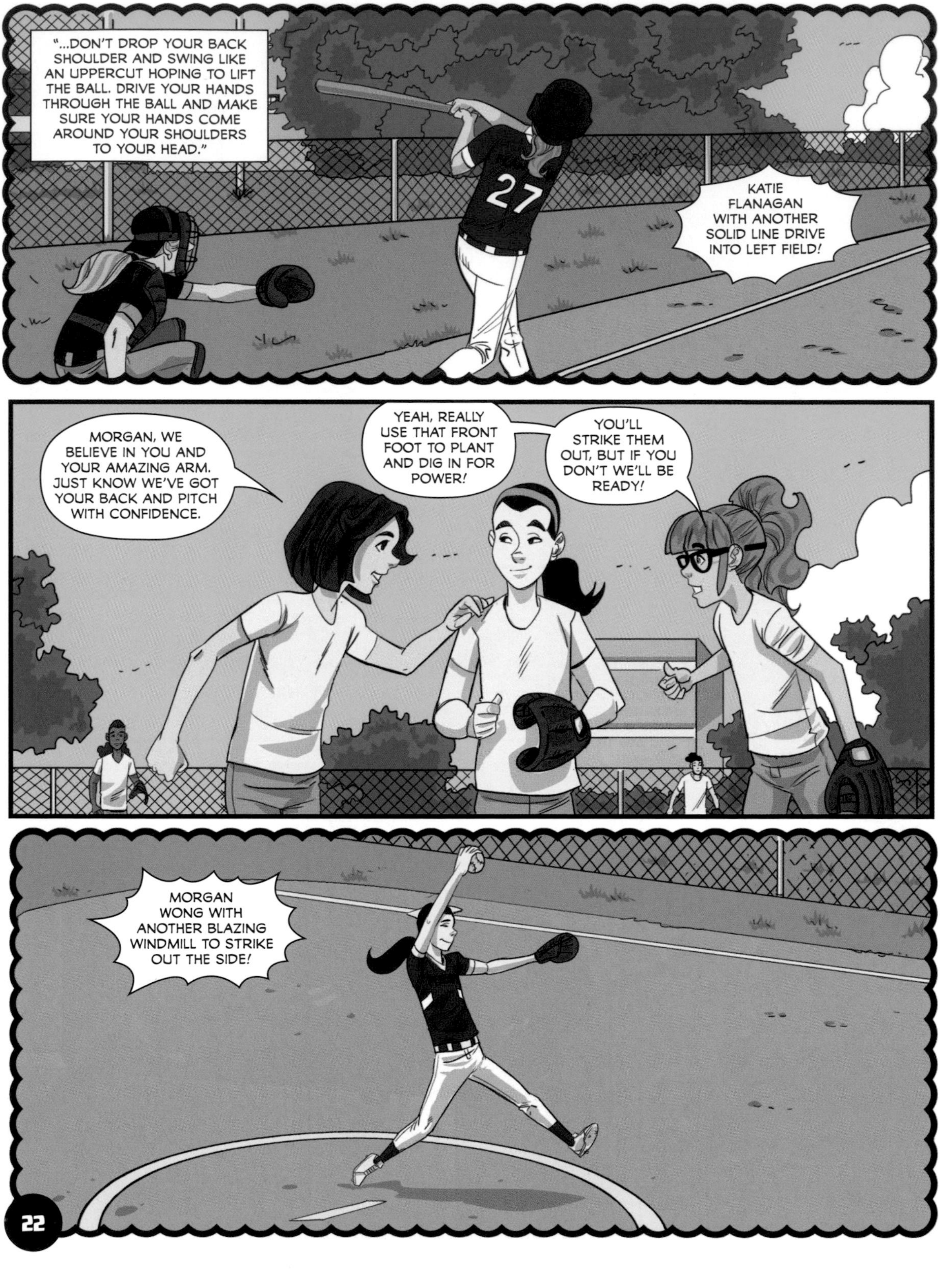
"...DON'T DROP YOUR BACK SHOULDER AND SWING LIKE AN UPPERCUT HOPING TO LIFT THE BALL. DRIVE YOUR HANDS THROUGH THE BALL AND MAKE SURE YOUR HANDS COME AROUND YOUR SHOULDERS TO YOUR HEAD."
27
KATIE FLANAGAN WITH ANOTHER SOLID LINE DRIVE INTO LEFT FIELD!
MORGAN, WE BELIEVE IN YOU AND YOUR AMAZING ARM. JUST KNOW WE'VE GOT YOUR BACK AND PITCH WITH CONFIDENCE.
YEAH, REALLY USE THAT FRONT FOOT TO PLANT AND DIG IN FOR POWER!
YOU'LL STRIKE THEM OUT, BUT IF YOU DON'T WE'LL BE READY!
MORGAN WONG WITH ANOTHER BLAZING WINDMILL TO STRIKE OUT THE SIDE!

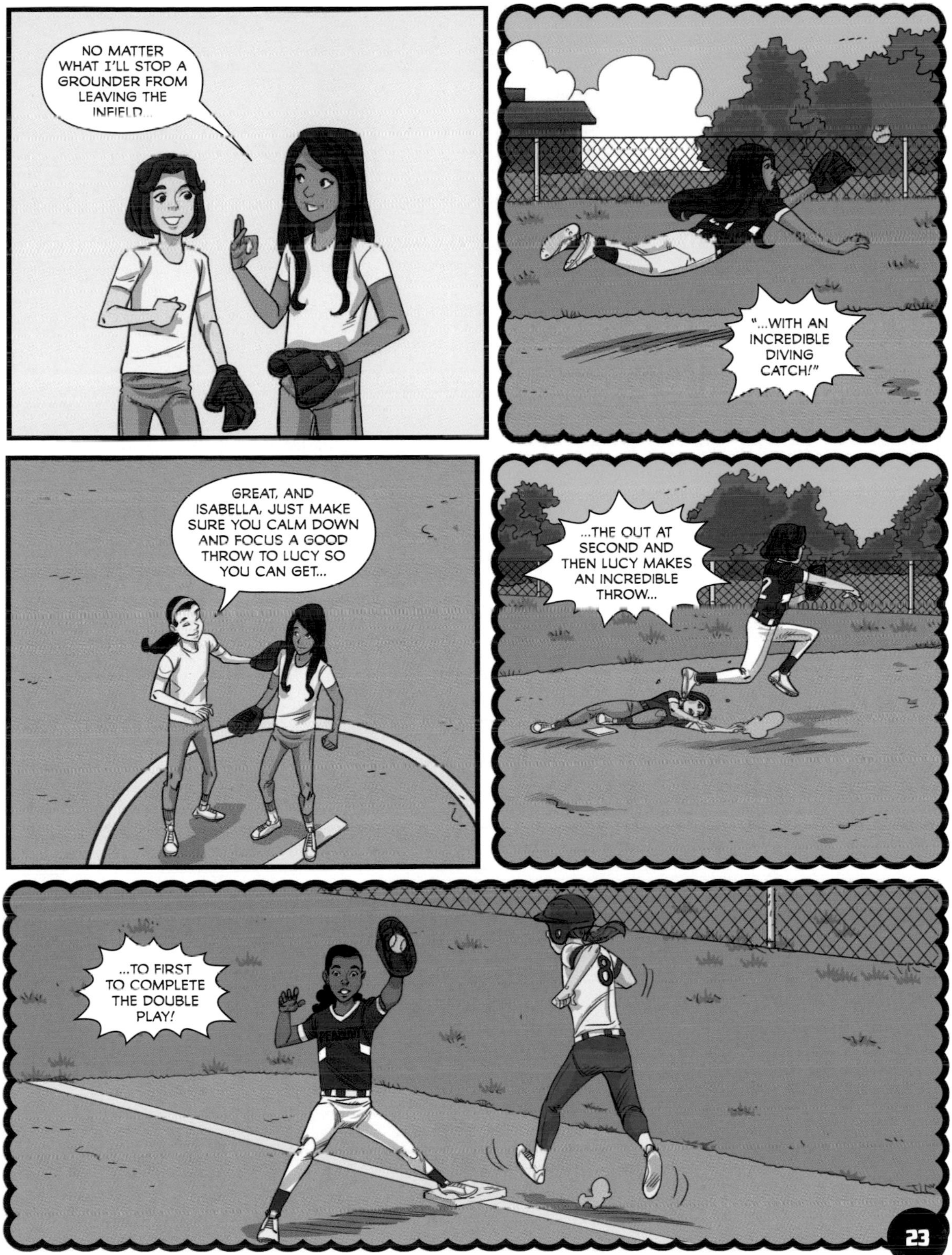
NO MATTER WHAT I'LL STOP A GROUNDER FROM LEAVING THE INFIELD...
"...WITH AN INCREDIBLE DIVING CATCH!"
GREAT, AND ISABELLA, JUST MAKE SURE YOU CALM DOWN AND FOCUS A GOOD THROW TO LUCY SO YOU CAN GET...
...THE OUT AT SECOND AND THEN LUCY MAKES AN INCREDIBLE THROW...
...TO FIRST TO COMPLETE THE DOUBLE PLAY!

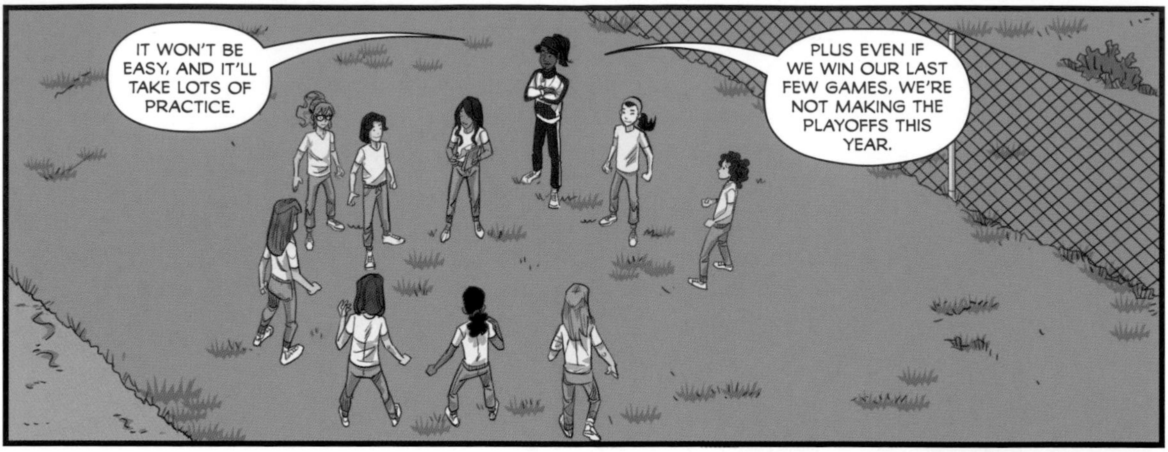
IT WON'T BE EASY, AND IT'LL TAKE LOTS OF PRACTICE.
PLUS EVEN IF WE WIN OUR LAST FEW GAMES, WE'RE NOT MAKING THE PLAYOFFS THIS YEAR.

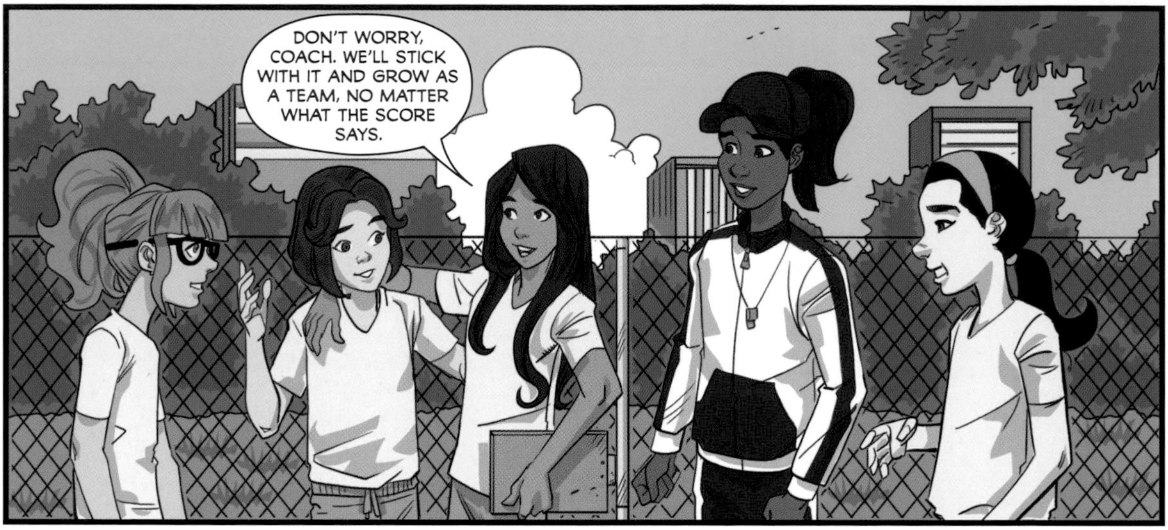
DON'T WORRY, COACH. WE'LL STICK WITH IT AND GROW AS A TEAM, NO MATTER WHAT THE SCORE SAYS.

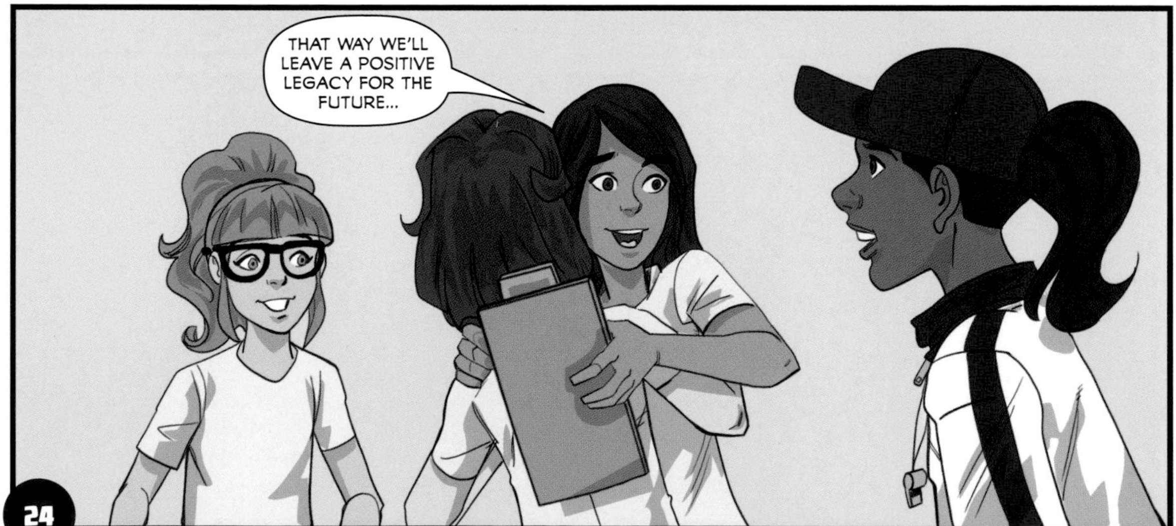
THAT WAY WE'LL LEAVE A POSITIVE LEGACY FOR THE FUTURE...

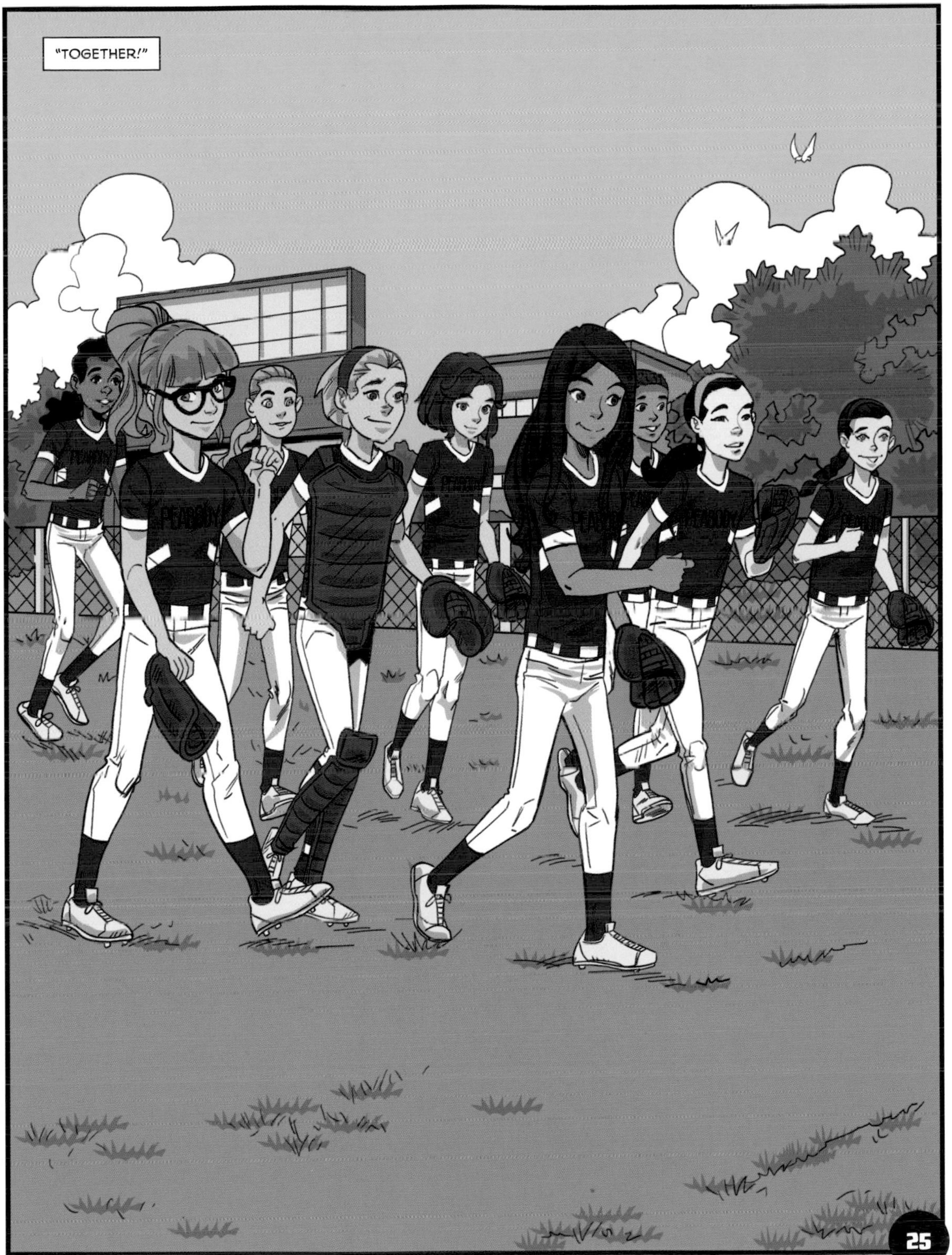
"TOGETHER!"
PEABODY

ISABELLA &

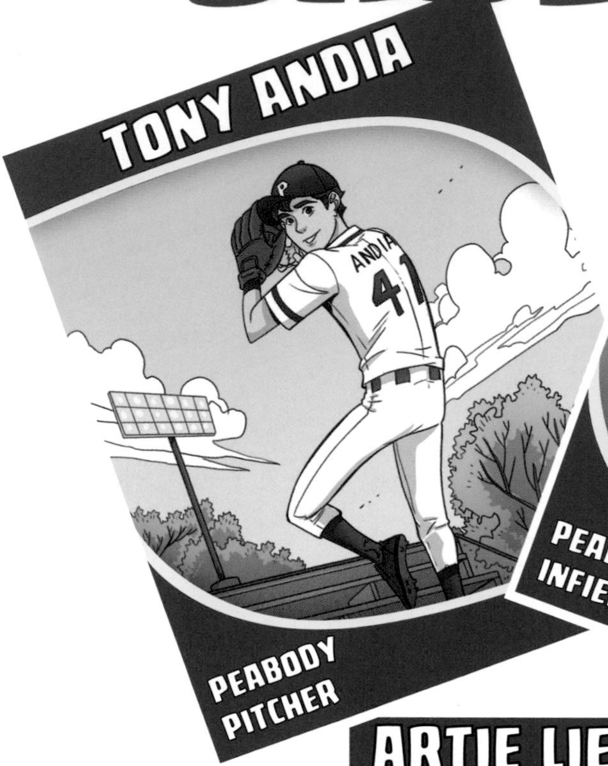
TONY ANDIA
ANDIA
PEABODY
PITCHER

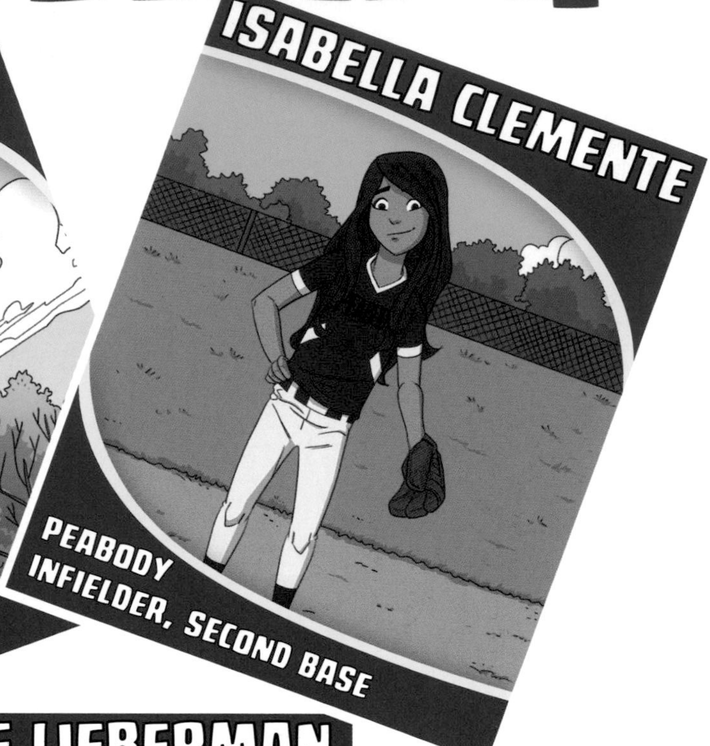
ISABELLA CLEMENTE
PEABODY
INFIELDER, SECOND BASE

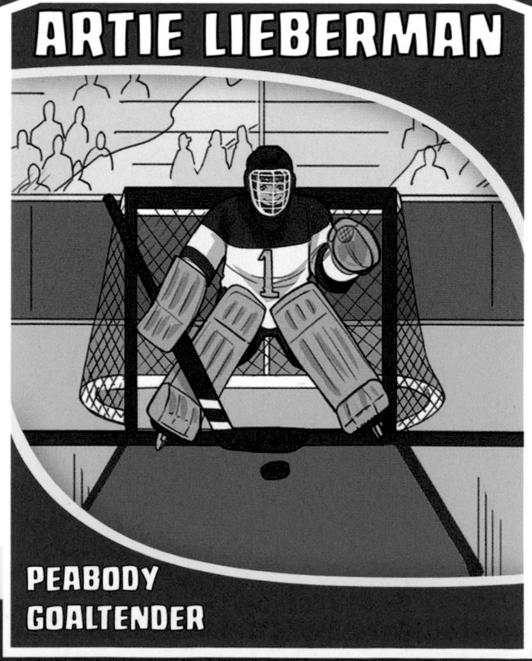
ARTIE LIEBERMAN
PEABODY
GOALTENDER

FRIENDS

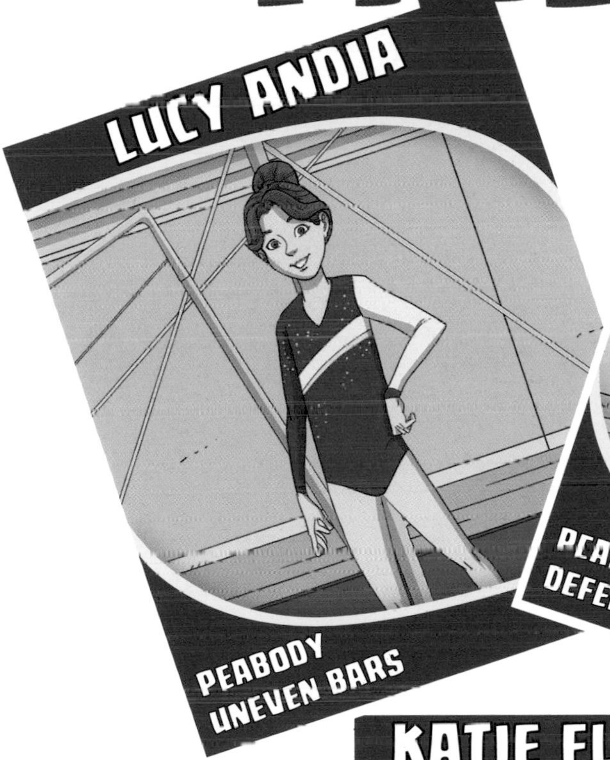
LUCY ANDIA
PEABODY
UNEVEN BARS

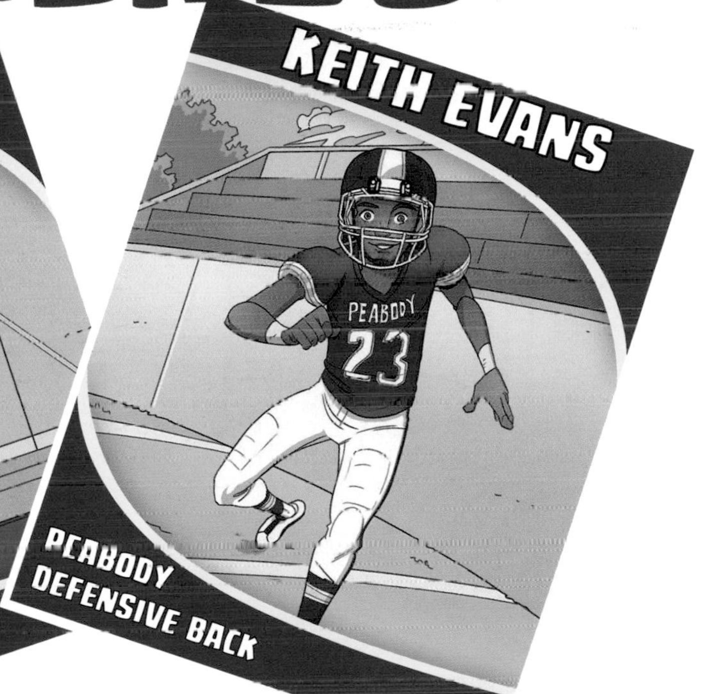
KEITH EVANS
PEABODY
23
PEABODY
DEFENSIVE BACK

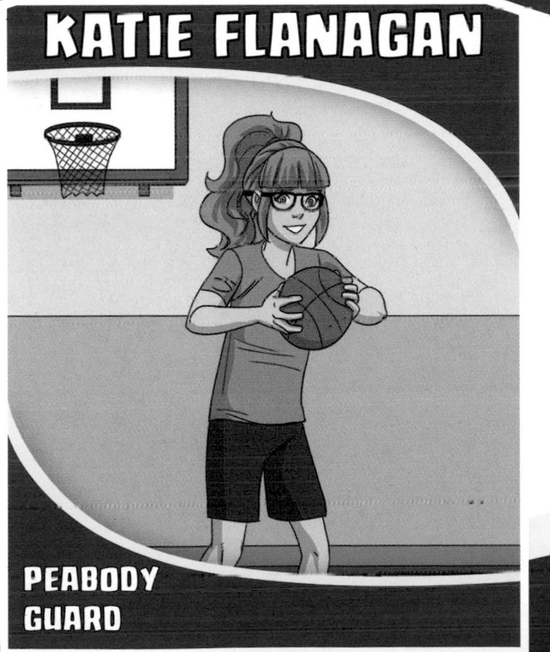
KATIE FLANAGAN
PEABODY
GUARD

SOFTBALL

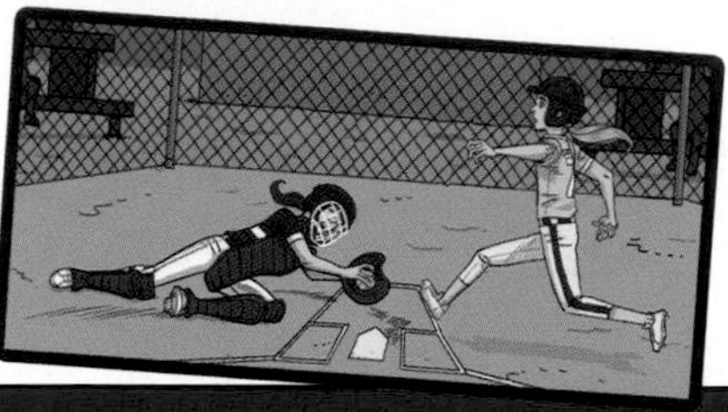

1. There are 9 innings in a baseball game. How many are in a standard fast pitch softball game?

a. 5
b. 7
c. 9
d. 1

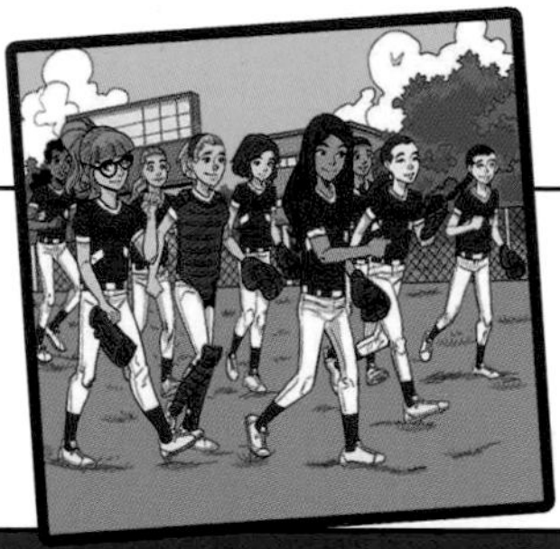

2. A baseball can be compared to an orange at 9 inches (22.8 cm) in circumference. What is the circumference of a softball?

a. 1 inch (2.5 cm) like a blueberry
b. 2 inches (5 cm) like a grape
c. 12 inches (30 cm) like a grapefruit
d. 18 inches (45.7) like a pineapple

3. A baseball bat can be no longer than 42 inches (106 cm) in length. What is the maximum length of a softball bat?

a. 40 inches (101 cm)
b. 35 inches (89 cm)
c. 45 inches (114 cm)
d. 34 inches (86 cm)

4. Which action is allowed in fast pitch softball but not in slow pitch?

a. squeeze play
b. home run
c. double play
d. stolen base

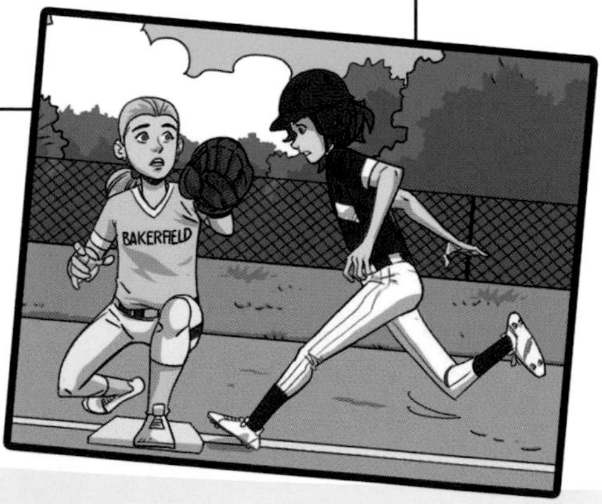
BAKERFIELD

5. Softball was invented in the United States. In which city did it originate?

a. Los Angeles
b. Chicago
c. Missoula
d. Oklahoma City

QUIZ

6. The United States had a long winning streak in the Olympics between 2000 and 2008. How many games in a row did they win?

a. 8
b. 14
c. 18
d. 22

7. What swing is allowed in baseball and fast pitch softball, but not permitted in slow pitch softball?

a. home run
b. check
c. chop
d. bunt

8. How many times has Team USA won Olympic gold in women's fast pitch softball?

a. 1
b. 2
c. 3
d. 4

9. In the four Olympics in which softball was played prior to its discontinuation, the United States won three gold medals. Which country won the fourth?

a. China
b. Canada
c. Japan
d. Kenya

10. What year did the name softball first become used for the sport?

a. 1886
b. 1926
c. 1996
d. 2006

29

* Answers on page 32

WHAT DO YOU THINK?

The pressure to win can sometimes make people lose focus on things that matter. Success can be measured in growth, improvement, and building others up, not just by who holds the trophy in the end.

- Describe the pressure Isabella felt as her team's leader. Have you ever felt pressure as a leader? How can a leader's attitude, positive or negative, affect those around them?

- Isabella blamed Lucy for missing a play when she was actually at fault. Describe a time when you didn't take responsibility for a mistake you made. What happened? How can you avoid a similar situation in the future?

- Describe a time when you were on a team with a losing record. Were you able to still enjoy games? Why or why not? What did you learn from that season?

- Isabella allowed losing to affect how she treated her friends. Have you ever struggled with something and let it affect your relationships? How did you make things better?

- A winning legacy isn't always a winning record. Sometimes it is a foundation for future growth. Describe a time you taught someone younger than you. What did you learn from the process of mentoring?

SOFTBALL FUN FACTS

1. Softball began in 1887 as an indoor sport! Over time, it has been called kitten ball, mush ball, and playground ball.

2. Softball became an Olympic sport at the 1996 summer games in Atlanta, Georgia. It was discontinued after the 2008 games in Bejing, China, but was reinstated for the 2020 games in Tokyo, Japan.

3. In slow pitch softball, the ball must be thrown underhand in an arc that ranges from six to twelve feet (2 to 4m) off the ground. However, in fast pitch softball there are no speed, arc, or curve restrictions.

4. There is a verison of slow pitch softball that uses a 16-inch (40.6-cm) ball, and the fielders typically play without gloves!

5. Jennie Finch is one of the best players in softball history. She won the 2001 Women's College World Series, a gold medal at the 2004 Olympics, and a silver medal at the 2008 Olympics. Her fastball is so fast she has struck out Major Leage Baseball players Albert Pujols, Mike Piazza, and Brian Giles!

GLOSSARY

bloop single – A weakly hit fly ball that drops in between an infielder and an outfielder for a single.

bottom of the order – The seventh, eighth, and ninth batters in the batting order. These players usually contribute more as defensive players than as hitters.

double play – A defensive play in which two offensive players are put out as a result of a continous action from one at bat.

dynasty – When one team wins multiple championships in a row over several seasons.

legacy – Something transmitted by or received from an ancestor or someone from the past.

ANSWERS

1. b   2. c   3. d   4. d   5. b   6. c   7. d   8. c   9. d   10. b

ONLINE RESOURCES

Booklinks
NONFICTION NETWORK
FREE! ONLINE NONFICTION RESOURCES

To learn more about softball, sportsmanship, and teamwork, please visit **abdobooklinks.com** or scan this QR code. These links are routinely monitored and updated to provide the most current information available.